2·99

PAST TENSE

Sheila Spencer-Smith

Scripture Union
130 City Road, London EC1V 2NJ

For Karina

© Sheila Spencer-Smith 1993
First published 1993

ISBN 0 86201 771 8

British Library Cataloguing-in-Publication Data.
A catalogue record for this book is available from the British Library.

Phototypeset by Intype, London
Printed and bound in Great Britain by Cox and Wyman Ltd, Reading.

~1~

Lauren saw their car as she neared the corner. It had been reversed into their drive, and a flash of sunlight caught the front window. Dad wasn't usually home this early, she thought as she swung her school-bag up in her arms so she could run more easily. He had never been as early as this since he'd gone back to work after Mum died.

She reached the front gate, and then stopped, breath-less. Everything looked the same . . . the same orange marigolds in the white tub, the same roses sprawled over the side fence, the same peeling blue paint on the front door. She had panicked unnecessarily. Dad was home early so that he could take her uncle to Bristol bus station to catch the coach for Heathrow. How could she have forgotten that Uncle Dave was going back to Canada today and wanted her to see him off on the first stage of his long journey?

Feeling a little foolish, she looked around her. Relieved that no one had noticed her mad rush, she hitched up her bag again and felt in her pocket for her key before she remembered that she wasn't going to need it today.

Even before she opened the back door she heard the loud voices and knew at once that something was wrong after all. Her father's Yorkshire accent was more pronounced than usual while her uncle's booming tones sounded apologetic.

'I had to tell him,' Uncle Dave was saying. 'The boy is Sue's son. He has a right to know his natural mother's dead, and . . .'

Lauren went in, her mouth dry. The clock on the wall chimed four times into deep, sudden silence.

'What's wrong?' she cried. 'Mum's son? But she didn't have a son!'

Two faces stared at her, Dad's white and drawn and her uncle's puffy and flushed.

She pushed a strand of fine hair away from her troubled eyes. For a moment no one spoke. She let her bag thud to the floor, and took a deep, rasping breath. 'Dad, what's the matter? What's Uncle Dave on about? What does he mean . . . Mum's son?'

Her father cleared his throat. 'You see . . . I promised Mum not to tell you.' A shiver seemed to go through his body. 'But now you've overheard some of it, and you'll have to know. Your mother . . . she was married and divorced before we met. She wanted to start afresh, to forget it ever happened. That's why I promised never to mention it to you.'

'And the son . . . ?'

Uncle Dave spoke gruffly. 'I couldn't go back home to Toronto not saying anything about what I did. He had to know. It's only right.'

She stared at him. The untidy shelves behind him must be seen to, she thought. They were never like that before Mum died. She must start on them as soon as Uncle

4

Dave had left so they would look the same as they used to . . .

'There's more to tell you, lass, about the boy.' Her father spoke in such a low voice she could hardly hear him.

And she didn't want to hear him. She concentrated her whole attention on the messy shelves behind his dark head, trying to shut out what he was trying to tell her.

'Lauren!' Dad was speaking in his old forceful way again now, willing her to listen. 'Mum had a child, a boy. He was two when she was divorced and left him.'

Perplexed, she tried hard to focus on what he was saying. 'Mum had a little boy and she went away and left him?' she said, unbelieving. She gave her uncle a startled glance and saw that he had moved to the window and was standing with his back to the light, clenching his hands.

'Oh no, she wouldn't have done anything like that. Not my mum.' Lauren's voice broke on a sob and she struggled hard to swallow back the tears.

There was an instant's icy silence. Then Lauren flew to her father, and was immediately pulled hard against him and held tight. His warm jersey was comforting. Here was safety as it always had been ever since she could remember.

But she couldn't blot out her uncle's voice. 'All the time I've been over here I've been trying to make up my mind what to do. Your mum was my sister, Lauren, but I've no right to butt in. That's what I thought at first. But they ought to know, you see, her first family. They ought to be told. So I wrote to the grandparents' address in York. The father took the boy abroad when he and your mum split up, but they may be home now. In any case they'll get the message.'

Lauren pulled away from her father, and stood glaring at him, her brown eyes enormous. 'First family! We're her family, Dad and me.'

She felt the warning pressure of her father's hand on her shoulder. 'Leave it now, lass. Uncle Dave's got a coach to catch. OK? We must go now. Are you coming?'

Her uncle gave her a worried smile. 'You'll come and see me off, Lauren, love? I'd like you to.'

She nodded. 'I've got to change first.'

Her father gave her a slight push towards the door, and she was out of it and upstairs to her room in a flash. Pulling off her school uniform she slipped into T-shirt and jeans, her uncle's words going round and round inside her head. She didn't believe what he said. She wouldn't believe it. Snatching up her comb she pulled it through her hair, and stared at the white face looking back at her from the mirror. Malicious lies, she thought, all of it, and her warm-hearted mother was no longer here to tell them so.

Downstairs again, she said nothing more to Uncle Dave. He was silent, too, as they drove to the town centre. She stared out of the car window, unconscious of everything except Dad's voice, a tone deeper than usual, talking of ordinary things.

As soon as the coach left, her father caught hold of Lauren's arm and propelled her towards the cafeteria. 'Coffee's what we need. It'll do us both good.'

Seated opposite him at the table in the window, she took a deep breath. 'What are we going to do, Dad?' she asked bleakly.

He gave her a quick smile that warmed his eyes for a moment. His dark hair looked bedraggled on his fore-head, and she wanted to comfort him and make things right. He raised his cup to his lips and then put it down again. 'Mum was a good wife to me, and a good mother to you, Lauren. Never forget that.'

'As if I could!' she burst out. 'That's what makes it so . . . so . . .'

'I know, lass.' Her father's voice was so full of compassion she could hardly bear it. This news was a shock for him too. 'I'd put it right out of my mind, like Mum wanted.'

'Why didn't Uncle Dave say something when he first came over this time?' she wailed. 'It's eleven whole months since the accident and Mum died.'

'It was a hard decision for him to make. He had to be sure he was doing this for the best.'

She took a gulp of hot coffee. 'So this is best . . . raking up the past, telling me about it now? Suppose they come looking for us, the boy and his father? What shall we do then?'

Her father leaned across the table and clasped her hands in his. 'Come now, think on it. The child was two, and his dad took him off abroad to live. It'll not mean owt to him.'

'So why tell him then?'

'Dave had to do what he felt was right and we must accept it.'

'If only we could go right away from here,' she said, pulling her hands away. 'We nearly did when you were made redundant.'

Mr Wainwright sighed. 'Your mother didn't fancy moving back north when I got the offer of the warden's job at that adventure centre in North Yorkshire. You can see why now. York's a long way from Alderdale, but even so. Anyway the Wildlife Trust job here seemed right for me at the time and we decided to stay put.' He glanced at his watch. 'Aren't you playing badminton tonight?'

Lauren drank the last of her coffee, and sprang up. 'I promised to meet Vicki at the sports centre, and I forgot. She'll be waiting for me there!'

Her father got to his feet, too. 'I'll drop you off on the way home. Too late to play yourself but a bit of company will do you good. You'll come home on the bus?'

Lauren nodded, and pushed back her hair. She badly needed to talk to her friend. Even so she didn't say a word to Vicki about Uncle Dave until they were at the bus stop on the way home. It came out haltingly at first and then she couldn't stop herself.

Her friend's plump, round face shone with interest as their bus came lumbering towards them and shuddered to a stop. She humped up her sports bag and followed Lauren up the stairs.

'I simply can't get over it,' Lauren whispered as they sank down together in the front seat.

Beside her Vicki sat stolidly, her bag wedged between her feet. Her frown made deep grooves in her forehead as she struggled to say the right thing. 'What will you do now your uncle's told them?'

Lauren shrugged. 'I don't know. I don't care. Anyway I don't believe it.'

There was silence between them as the bus negotiated a roundabout. 'I think you're lucky,' Vicki said at last.

'*Lucky*!'

'I always wanted a brother.'

Lauren sprang round as if shot. 'A brother?' It simply hadn't occurred to her that she had a brother. She took a deep breath. 'But I don't want a brother. We were a real family on our own, Mum and Dad and me.'

Vicki looked at her curiously. 'Don't you want to know what he's like?'

'Never!'

'I would if I was you.'

Lauren turned to look out of the window at the freshly-planted shrubs outside the newest buildings on the industrial estate, thinking that Vicki was no help. She didn't understand. It made her feel lonely.

Into her mind came pictures from the past . . . her mother laughing on the beach at Porthcarne, picking up her five-year-old self and spinning her round in a haze of sparkling warmth. The memories came crowding in and wouldn't stop . . . her first morning at infants' school and Mum's anxious, caring face at the window as if she couldn't bear to let her little child out of her sight . . .

Lauren shuddered. It was all pretence, all lies. It had to be if what Uncle Dave told her was true. It didn't mean anything any more. The past was all changed because of Uncle Dave's words. It was all different from how she remembered it.

Vicki sat back in her seat, alarmed at the expression on her face. 'So what will you do?' she asked.

Lauren hunched her shoulders in a firm, unyielding line. Her mother was like a stranger now. She hadn't really known her, not how she had really been. Everything was changed. How was it possible for her to desert her little son like that and not tell anybody? It made her, Lauren Wainwright, into a different person too, and one she didn't know either.

The bus drew to a halt by a row of shops.

'Come on, Lauren,' Vicki said, hauling up her bag and crashing to the head of the stairs.

Lauren looked down at the shops and the top of the

sycamore tree as if she would never see them again. Her nostrils were full of the warm, sickly, bus smell as she followed Vicki down to the lower deck and waited for the other passengers to shuffle their way off.

~2~

'Dad, please, I really mean it.'

Mr Wainwright gave an exaggerated sigh, and grinned down at Lauren. He'd been on the point of making himself some tea when she'd come bursting into the kitchen. He paused with the empty kettle in his hand. 'Now wait a minute,' he said, half-laughing. 'Not so fast.'

'Don't you see, Dad, it makes sense. If we move away no one can check up on us because they won't know where we are.'

The lines in his forehead deepened. 'You'd run away?'

Lauren looked back at him, serious-eyed and frowning a little. 'It doesn't look that way to me, Dad. You're my family, no one else. I don't *want* anyone else. Think what a challenge it would be for both of us to go to that adventure place in North Yorkshire! You said the job as warden's been re-advertised. It's eleven months since Mum died. Things are different now.'

'Now hold on a minute, lass. It needs thinking on.'

'Not for me it doesn't.' Lauren removed her jacket and placed it carefully on the back of the chair before sinking down at the kitchen table.

'I've been considering,' her father said as he sat down opposite her and rested both elbows on the table. 'He's your half-brother, that boy. Like it or not, it's a fact. Why not give it a chance if he wants to contact you?'

The colour flew to Lauren's face. 'Never! I'll have nothing to do with him, ever. And I won't believe Mum was the sort of person to . . .' She broke off, tears choking her, and plunged her face in her hands. When she looked up again, her father was staring at the kettle on the table in front of him as if he'd never seen it before.

She leapt up. 'I'll make the tea,' she said more calmly.

'Better get off to bed as soon as you've drunk it. OK? You look all in.'

He looked as if he could do with an early night himself, Lauren thought, as she carried their empty cups to the sink to deal with them right away. It had hit him hard too. She hesitated, wondering whether to say any more and then deciding against it.

Upstairs in her bedroom, she knew there was no point in rushing. She wouldn't sleep tonight with Uncle Dave's revelations hanging over her. Impossible to believe his terrible words, even though everything pointed to them being true. But she'd have nothing to do with Mum's first family. *First* family! That's what Uncle Dave said, and that's what hurt.

Lauren sank down on the bed. She took deep, calming breaths, wondering for the first time if her uncle had been living in this country at the time and had actually met the boy. He'd gone to Canada soon afterwards probably, but he might just have known him. Had Mum sworn him to secrecy? It seemed likely. But to spill it all out now . . . it was cruel!

Mum was such a caring person. A little boy . . . to go away and leave him. How could she?

Lauren gave a great shudder as she got up stiffly. Stretching, she walked to the window and threw it wide open to stare out at the small back garden. Mum had loved flowers, and had taken such pleasure in her roses and delphiniums.

She gave a loud sob. It didn't matter if she gave way and cried because there was no one to hear her. The television was on downstairs and Dad wouldn't be up for ages.

At last she raised her head, and wiped her face roughly on her sleeve. As she got ready to slip into bed she thought of Vicki, who wanted her to find out about her brother.

Vicki had seemed different this evening, and she felt different herself, too, because of what Uncle Dave had come out with. Memories of Mum could never be the same again. All her values were changed, and she felt bereft because of it.

They *had* to start a new life somewhere else, she and Dad. There was no help for it if she wanted to find out who she really was . . .

Lauren slept, after a while, until the telephone's insistent ringing had her leaping out of bed and down the stairs at a gallop. Even then she stared at the receiver in shivering apprehension before she picked it up. The relief of it being a wrong number left her shaking.

'What is it, Lauren?' her father's deep voice asked from behind her.

He grabbed her in a bear hug for the time it took to compose herself. 'It's all right,' she said with only a slight quiver in her voice. 'It wasn't . . . A wrong number, that's all.'

As he released her she saw the anxiety in his face. 'You look pale, lass. Get back to bed, OK? It's a shock when the phone wakes you.'

That's what it was, a shock, she thought as she pulled her duvet over her head and tried to relax. But not the kind of shock Dad thought. It was the shock of fearing someone would try to contact her, someone she had sworn never to meet.

The postman came while they were eating their cereal and toast at the kitchen table. Lauren heard the letterbox rattle, and sat quite still as her father scraped back his chair and got up. She could hardly breathe as he returned with a brown envelope in his hand.

He sat down, and picked up the teapot.

'Aren't you going to open the letter, Dad?' she asked in a faint voice.

'Is anything wrong, lass?'

She shook her head, but he looked at her suspiciously as he finished pouring his tea.

He was maddeningly slow in slitting open the envelope and pulling out the typewritten sheets. A smile twitched his lips as he read, and the lines at the side of his eyes crinkled as he looked up. 'It's not a wrong number this time.'

She swallowed, and pushed back a stray lock of hair from her forehead. 'What is it?'

'Notification of the Ecology Society Meeting on Wednesday night. You'll be out, won't you Lauren, at the end of term disco?'

She let out an imperceptible sigh of relief. Would it always be like this now, with the overhanging fear of Mum's past catching up with them?

14

Once she would have had a great time at the disco, but not now. As she and Vicki went into the hall on Wednesday night she thought suddenly: I shouldn't be here. Not now. Not feeling like I don't belong any more.

No use saying anything more to Vicky about her gnawing wish to get right away. When she'd told her about the chance earlier, Vicki had thought her crazy.

She left early, and found her father home before her.

He looked up at her from behind his newspaper. 'I'll make an appointment with your year tutor, OK?' he said.

It sounded as if he was continuing a conversation begun earlier, but neither of them had mentioned the post of Warden of Alderdale Adventure Centre since the night Uncle Dave left. But that's how it was with Dad, Lauren thought. He got on the same wavelength with you immediately.

'Other people change schools a year before GCSE and it's all right,' she said stiffly, turning her back.

'I'll have a word with her, in case the job isn't permanent. See what she says. No good going on like this, jumping out of your skin every time the phone rings.'

She spun round, looking at him in wonder. 'You'd really change jobs just for me?'

He grinned and his rugged face lit as it always did when he was having a joke with her. He wasn't joking now, though. She could tell by the serious twist to his mouth. 'Not for you, lass, for me. It would be a rewarding job helping to run an adventure centre. Let's see what Miss Thingummy says about your education first, though, before we jump the gun. OK?'

Lauren smiled. 'OK.'

After that everything happened. It seemed amazing to

Lauren, on the last morning ten days later, that it had all been arranged so easily. Well, not exactly easily. It wasn't easy saying goodbye to Vicki and trying to explain that Dad was going to be Warden of the Alderdale Adventure Centre for a trial period of six weeks, the length of the summer holidays.

'So you'll be back for next term?' Vicki said, her eyes brightening.

But Lauren had to dash her hopes, and say that they expected to stay at Alderdale permanently if all went well. It was hard seeing her friend's disappointed expression.

'You'll come and stay, won't you, Vicki?' she asked anxiously. 'If you don't get fixed up with a holiday job of course.'

Vicki had smiled bleakly, not promising.

Now, with all the packing done, Lauren felt a moment's panic. She wasn't fooled for a moment by Dad's statement that their moving north was for his benefit. It was her decision, and the responsibility was heavy.

She pulled her bulging rucksack across to the door and leant it against her case. Then she shrugged her slim shoulders. She could cope. She *would* cope!

All the same she had more doubts as they piled the luggage into the car and stuffed every available space with the odds and ends they needed to take. It was strange leaving their home behind and going to an unknown destination. Neither of them had asked what the Warden's quarters would be like.

'Do you think it'll be a house or a flat, Dad?' she asked as they joined the M5 and speeded north up the motorway.

'Who knows?' said her father, a smile touching his lips

as he stared straight ahead. 'A bungalow, a barn, a tent?'

Then she was smiling too. 'A lighthouse, a windmill, a houseboat?'

'A cave, a cellar, a ruined castle?'

'I know,' she said enthusiastically. 'A modern block of flats!'

'That's it,' he said. 'Just the thing. Anyway we'll have to wait and see. All we know is it's furnished. Just as well in the circumstances.'

They had left their house just as it was, furniture and all. They would decide later what was to be done with it.

Lauren gave a little giggle. 'We're bound to be living in one of them unless we can think of anything else.'

It was a ruined cottage. At least, that's what it looked like as they drove past it, down the drive bordered with banks of heather, when they reached Alderdale at last.

The Adventure Centre buildings themselves were modern, built on the hillside above a wide stretch of water with more heathery hills beyond. The fresh moorland air hit them like a polar blast as they opened the car doors and got out. Mr Wainwright stretched, and then let out a long breath.

'Here at last,' he said in satisfaction.

Someone was coming out to meet them, a tall boy whose dark hair grew in tufts at the back giving him a look of someone much younger. He must be at least seventeen, Lauren thought, retreating a little; perhaps even eighteen, the same age as the boy who was supposed to be her brother. For a moment she had the strangest feeling, as if he had suddenly materialised in front of her. Then she took a deep breath too, and tried to smile.

'Mr Wainwright?' the boy asked in a deep tone that got lighter as he went on. 'I'm Ben Adams. My mother's the catering manager. That's her official title, but she does all sorts. She told me to look out for you.'

'My daughter, Lauren,' he said.

Although shorter than Ben her father looked solid and safe, Lauren thought as she moved closer to him.

The boy nodded to her, a faint tinge of colour in his cheeks. 'That's where you'll be living,' he said, pointing up the hill behind them to the cottage they'd passed on their way down.

Her father nodded too, as if it was a normal thing to take up residence in a tumbledown ruin, but Lauren had other ideas.

'You don't mean to say we're going to live there?' she asked in horror. 'It's just an empty shell.' The worry of it almost took her breath away.

Ben's slow smile did nothing to dispel her doubts. She was responsible for them being here and leaving their comfortable house. At least she had expected somewhere decent to live. She was nearly in tears as they struggled up the path with the suitcases, Ben in front and her father behind.

They dumped them outside as Ben pushed open the rickety door. Inside was a long stone passage that struck chill into Lauren's heart. On the left was a sort of living-room with part converted into a kitchen.

'We made two rooms into one,' Ben said almost apologetically. 'As you can see it's an open fire for heating, but there's plenty of fuel . . . logs mostly.'

As Lauren moved nearer to the fire she could see that the furniture was adequate – a wooden table and chairs and a dresser. There was even a sofa and a couple of easy chairs in brown flowered material to match the curtains. She shivered, in spite of the warmth. It was like winter.

'The two bedrooms are on the ground floor, too,' Ben

said, shuffling his feet on the rough matting. 'Nothing's been done with upstairs. That's why the stairs are boarded up and it looks like a ruin from outside. It's not quite as bad as that.' He shot a smile in Lauren's direction, but she ignored it.

'No bathroom?' she asked. Her voice was like ice, and she was glad to see the colour flood his cheeks.

'We'll discover that for ourselves in a minute or two,' her father said. 'Let's get the cases in now, and get settled.'

But before they could do anything about it there was a gentle tap at the door and a voice said: 'I hope my son's been doing the honours for me. Sorry I couldn't be here at once. I'm Grace Adams.'

'Arnold Wainwright,' Lauren's father said, real warmth in his voice as he took her hand in a firm grip.

She smiled, and her pale face seemed to light up for a moment. Then she rubbed both hands down the sides of her faded jeans, and turned to Lauren.

'I'm glad to see you, dear,' she said. 'I expect you're a great help to your father.'

There was something about her fair looks that had Lauren smiling back at her. This small woman looked much too young to be Ben Adams' mother.

'Well, I won't keep you. No doubt you'll want to get settled. Come down to the main building when you're ready, and I'll show you round.' She made as if to withdraw, and looked enquiringly at her son.

Ben flushed. 'I'll be off then?'

'Come back later if you like,' said Mr Wainwright. 'OK? You can show Lauren round a bit. She'll be glad of some young company.'

'I'll be all right,' Lauren said, moving further away and standing with her back to the wall. She didn't want company. She wanted to be on her own with Dad, just the two of them.

Ben shuffled his feet, and then rushed for the door ahead of his mother who looked round to smile at them before leaving them to their own devices.

'So . . . what do you think of it?' Mr Wainwright asked as he hauled the suitcases inside. 'Not bad, is it?'

Lauren wrinkled her nose.

He grinned at her, and ruffled her hair. 'I'll get the rest of the stuff out of the car.'

While he was gone Lauren investigated further. The two small bedrooms, sparsely furnished with bed and wardrobe, were at the side of the cottage that looked over the lake. There was a door at the end of the chilly passage that led out at the back almost into the hillside. Near it, but not joined to the building, was the bathroom. It looked as if it had been made out of an outhouse, but was clean and neat with more of the dull matting on the floor. The green bath with the shower unit above it, washbasin and toilet were new.

Thank goodness for that, she thought. All the same she didn't fancy finding her way out here by torchlight in the dead of winter. But perhaps they wouldn't be here in winter. Then she remembered *why* they were here, and gave a little shiver. Whatever the place was like it was safe. A good place to forget.

She felt better when the unpacking was done and some of their own bits and pieces were scattered round the place. The passageway still felt cold, though. It was like a tunnel deep in the earth. Not until the door at the end was opened was there any light apart from the front door and in this weather it wouldn't be left open at all.

Her father made coffee while she finished unpacking, and then they were ready to go down to the Adventure

Centre and learn to find their way around this strange place.

It had all happened so swiftly Lauren hadn't had time to wonder what her own part in the scheme was going to be. Dad had concentrated on finding out about a school for her to attend in September if necessary, being flustered about the distance involved until he learnt about the school minibus that travelled the countryside picking people up. After that it was the details of his own new job that filled his mind, but nothing had been said about the part she was to play.

As they shut the cottage door behind them and set off down the track Lauren took a deep breath of moorland air. With a feeling of disquiet she saw Ben Adams waiting for them. Why couldn't he leave them alone? It was strange enough being in this different place without having him hanging round. She didn't want anyone else, couldn't he see that? They needed to get used to things on their own.

But her father was smiling at him, and asking questions about the group of young people who used the Adventure Centre and where they came from.

'They come from all over,' Ben said. He ran his hand through his dark hair making the back stand up in tufts which he smoothed down again. 'The committee places adverts in lots of local papers. Sometimes individual people come, but mostly it's organised groups. We've a church group coming in soon from Misterdale, near Newcastle. They come every year. The group in now are going home tomorrow.'

He smiled at Lauren, but she looked hurriedly away, not wanting to join in this discussion. They'd find out all these details soon enough, she supposed. Right now it was only necessary to see Dad's office and discover what time he was supposed to be there in the morning. It was getting late. They were both tired. Already the hills were dusky against the sky.

She gave a great yawn. Dad's deep voice seemed to be going round and round in a kind of vacuum.

'Time for bed,' she heard him say at last. 'See you in the morning then, Ben. OK?'

Lauren didn't see him go. He seemed to melt into the shadowy hillside, leaving her with a strange feeling she couldn't quite fathom.

'It'll seem better in the morning,' Mr Wainwright said. 'Not so bleak and far from civilisation.'

But that's what she wanted, Lauren thought, to be as far from civilisation as possible so she could sort herself out in the only way she could think of in the circumstances. It was a strange reason for being here helping to run an Adventure Centre, but that couldn't be helped.

She caught hold of her father's arm, and squeezed it. 'It's all right,' she said rather breathlessly. 'Don't worry, Dad, we'll cope.'

'That's my girl,' he said approvingly. 'We've got it in us, both of us. We'll not let owt get us down.'

~3~

Lauren thought of those words next morning when she peered out of her bedroom window. She couldn't even see the lake. Everything was blotted out by sheets of dreary rain.

She shivered. Who would think it was summer? Hastily she dressed in jeans and a thick jersey, and then went along the cold passage to the door at the end. Talk about roughing it, she thought as she pulled back the long bolt to let herself out. Well, she would have to get used to it. At least the bathroom was newly done even if it was only an outhouse. Back indoors again she was surprised to see the front door open.

'Dad?'

He came in like a breath of fresh air, shaking rain from his dark hair. 'I thought I'd have a look round on my own,' he said, wiping his feet on the mat. 'By, it's cold out there. Nobody about yet, and no wonder.' He bent to take off his boots to leave by the door, and then padded in his thick socks to the kitchen.

For some reason it seemed warmer in here this morning, maybe because it was so chilly outside. Lauren filled the kettle and plugged it in. Apart from coffee and biscuits last night, which they'd brought themselves with some other necessities, they hadn't bothered about anything else and were hardly conscious that the food cupboard and the fridge weren't empty.

She flung open the fridge door. 'Look Dad, food. Stacks of it . . . milk and butter and marge and cheese and tea, even some sausages and bacon!'

There was a granary loaf in the cupboard nearby, cereal and sugar.

'Ben's mother,' she said. 'She must have got food in for us.' Suddenly she felt ravenous, and much happier. She was eager now to get down to the clubhouse and see how it felt to be here in daylight.

The knock on the door made her jump.

Her father went to open it. 'The postman'll deliver all the Adventure Centre mail here from now on, to save taking it all the way down to the clubhouse.' He grinned as he placed a pile of letters on the table. 'Wants to save his legs, and who can blame him, specially today?'

It was still raining when they set off down the track, but not as much. Lauren could even see most of the lake now and a bit of the hills behind. There were people moving about between the clubhouse and the lake.

'They'll be the group packing up their tents,' her father said. 'Another lot are coming in a few days.'

He sounded confident, as if he couldn't wait to get started on the work he had to do to keep this place running. Lauren smiled. It was the best thing for him, to get stuck into something interesting to take his mind off other things.

They knew where his office was because it had been

pointed out to them last night. Now he went straight to it up the wooden staircase at the side of the building.

'Coming up?' he called, as Lauren hesitated. 'Or will you go and see what's going on elsewhere?'

She smiled at him as she saw his anxious look. 'I'll have a look around. See you later then.'

There was a lot more activity at the front of the club-house with people wandering about with clipboards and shouting directions, and the telephone ringing.

'The new chap'll answer it in the office,' a tall woman called in a deep, husky voice. Her brown eyes stared at Lauren from a long, pale face. Drops of rain clung to the wide shoulders of her navy anorak. 'So . . . you're Lauren, our new helper,' she said, when she had finished looking her up and down. 'You can give me a hand in the kitchen. I'm the programme organiser really, but we all muck in here.'

'Have a heart, Joanna.' Ben's mother came up to them with her hands full of tea-towels. 'Ben's around some-where, and it's stopped raining now. Lauren can help in the kitchen later.'

Lauren was grateful for her friendly smile. She didn't like the Joanna woman who shrugged her broad shoulders and turned away. She'd have to learn to work with them all, but just at the moment she wanted to get the feel of things.

Everyone was so busy it was hard not to feel out of it, though. She was relieved to see Ben running up the steps from the grass below where all the packing up was being done. A shaft of watery sunlight caught the top of his dark head for a moment.

'Ah Ben,' his mother said. 'I'd like you to do some-thing for me.'

A look passed between them. It was only a glance but

in it Lauren sensed the loving intimacy. It was like a shiver of pain deep inside her. So might her own mother have looked at her son if things hadn't gone tragically wrong. Since their arrival last night she'd put the thought of her half-brother out of her mind, but now it came flooding back with a poignancy that was terrible. He'd be Ben's age, near enough. Had Mum never thought of him all those years . . . wondered what he was doing, what he looked like?

The moment between Ben and his mother was over, but the memory of it lingered all the time Lauren was being shown the boatyard, and the stack of canoes at one side of it. She stared up at the masts of the sailing dinghies without seeing them because of the look on a mother's face as she looked at her son.

Had Mum ever looked at *her* like that? Since Uncle Dave's revelations it was hard to remember what it had been like, when all she could think of was that little abandoned two-year-old growing up without his mother. Maybe he was wondering about her now. Didn't you hear about people searching out their parents? There was nothing to stop him doing the same . . . except that Mum was dead.

She looked at Ben speculatively. He caught her look as he was tightening the cover on one of the boats, and a faint flush warmed his cheeks. He looked as if he expected her to be critical of him like last night.

'I'll need to take you round and show you what's what,' he said, obviously trying to be friendly. 'Later perhaps. Done any canoeing or caving before?'

'Caving?' she asked in astonishment.

He laughed and his brown eyes lit up. 'What do you think they come here for . . . sunbathing?'

Lauren rubbed her finger up and down the nylon

cover. 'Ben, you said about another group coming. Do you ever get people coming on their own?'

'Mmm. Sometimes, not often.'

'Have you got anyone coming who's booked in on their own?'

He shrugged. 'Your Dad will know. The booking lists are in his office. Why?'

Lauren turned away. 'It doesn't matter.' She couldn't ask Dad anyway. He'd know immediately what she was after, and she'd promised him she'd put it right out of her mind and concentrate on their new life. For his sake, too, she had to.

'The group'll just about be packed up now,' Ben said. 'They're off at eleven-thirty. Coming to say goodbye?'

They walked back up to the clubhouse. The large main room rattled with noise and laughter as the members of the group drank the coffee Joanna had made for them. She was smiling now, and her long face looked younger. All the time, though, she was glancing about her as if she was waiting for someone much more important to make an appearance.

'Who's she looking for?' Lauren asked Ben quietly as they fought their way to the serving hatch.

'That's just Joanna,' Ben whispered back. 'There's always someone more important round the next corner.'

He picked up two mugs of coffee and handed one to Lauren.

'It was kind of your mother to get us stocked up at the cottage,' Lauren said rather diffidently.

He looked pleased, and again a faint flush tinged his cheeks. 'We got the shopping yesterday morning. I ran Mum into Rawthwaite in the van, and we did it then.'

We, thought Lauren, sipping coffee. The two of them doing things together. Suddenly she couldn't bear the shine in Ben's eyes, or the way his mouth curved up at the corners. She banged down her half-empty mug, splashing coffee on the counter.

'Temper, temper!' Joanna threw an amused look at her as she reached for a cloth.

Lauren scowled. Then she turned and pushed her way out through the throng, running down the steps onto the grass. A couple of vans were drawn up on the paving stones nearby. Three men were loading up the equipment from the camp. Without thinking Lauren caught hold of a corner of a bundle and helped heave it across to the first van.

The man on the other end, short and stocky with a mass of red hair, grinned at her. 'Thanks, lass. You make ten of that lazy lot in there boozing coffee.'

Lauren smiled back. Though she didn't feel much like smiling, her companion's good temper was infectious. She picked up a milk crate filled with bottles of cleaning fluid and disinfectant.

'That's the ticket,' he said, beaming. 'Soon have it done at this rate.'

There was something soothing in the way he didn't ask questions or look at her at all. It made her feel she was part of the team and she liked the idea of doing something useful without being asked. Even the weight of some of the things she heaved across was helpful.

They had just finished when the hordes descended. Lauren stood back, watching everyone pile into the vans and wondering how there could possibly be room for them all.

A cheer went up as the two vans drove slowly up the track. An emptiness seemed to descend on the place when they had gone.

'Mum's looking for you,' Ben said at her side.

Lauren jumped.

'Are you all right?'

'What do you think?' she snapped. 'I don't have to stick glued to you all the time, do I?' She was sorry immediately, but it was too late. Ben had gone striding off, his back held straight. She hadn't meant to react like that. Ben was only being friendly, and she needed friends. Now he thought she hated him, and she couldn't blame him.

She found Grace in the clubhouse viewing the disorder, with a pucker of lines between her eyes. Joanna was nowhere to be seen, which was something, though her husky voice could be heard in the kitchen.

Grace's eyes lit up. 'Oh, there you are, love. I know it's boring for you, but could you see to this while I check the lists with your father? The brooms and things are in that cupboard by the hatch.'

She didn't wait for an answer. Left alone, Lauren opened the cupboard and removed a large broom and a duster. Although it looked as if a riot had taken place, Lauren found she enjoyed setting the room to rights. Once the chairs had been placed neatly under the tables and the floor swept, there wasn't much wrong that a damp cloth over the tables wouldn't put right.

She replaced the broom in the cupboard, and then went outside to the wooden balcony to shake her duster. The sun had broken through the clouds now and down below the lake sparkled. It even felt a couple of degrees warmer. One or two people were moving along the track to the boatyard and beneath the balcony some wooden picnic tables were being scraped across the paving stones.

Lauren wasn't conscious of the voices down below at first until the deep tones of Joanna caught her attention.

'Poor little waif,' she heard her say.

There were a few muttered words from another person, and then Joanna again: 'Not a bit like him, is she? So thin and wan. I shall take her in hand, put a bit of colour in those pale cheeks.' She gave a low gurgle. 'Think he'll be grateful to me?'

There was plenty of colour in Lauren's cheeks now. She stood quite still, gripping her duster.

The other person must have moved further away because Lauren couldn't hear what was said in reply. But Joanna's voice seemed to boom out as she speculated on the reason for their being here. 'They want looking after, the pair of them,' she said, her voice ringing with confidence. 'Poor lambs. Did you see how worn he looked? And that poor child needs mothering.'

There was no more, but for a moment Lauren couldn't move. She stared at the duster in her hand, all at once coming to life and shaking it over the balcony as if it was a declaration of war.

To her dismay Ben seemed to think it was a signal for him because he came springing up the steps as if he'd been waiting for it. He followed her into the clubhouse. 'Aren't you going to wipe the tables?' he said. 'Mum'll be after you if you don't.'

Lauren crashed open the kitchen door, found a damp cloth and attacked the tables as if they'd done her a great wrong. She had intended to show Ben she didn't mean what she'd said earlier, but now everything was going wrong again. She flicked back her hair as she finished, glaring at him.

'There's lunch to get now they've gone,' he said. 'Soup and bread and fruit. Afterwards I'll take you for a sail.'

'A sail? But I want to get the cottage sorted out a bit, and all our things arranged.'

Ben pushed a lock of dark hair off his forehead, glanced round the room and then back at her. 'You've done a lot this morning. Mum thought you'd like a break.'

'No thanks. So where's this soup then?'

Ben said nothing more as they prepared the food for the small group of them left, but his lips were tight as if he'd like to get back at her.

He kept well away from her as soon as the others appeared in the clubhouse, and she couldn't blame him. He pulled two tables together and placed the plate of bread and the bowl of fruit in the middle.

Carefully Lauren carried the casserole of soup in and placed it on the mat that Ben had set ready for it.

'Shall I serve?' Grace asked. 'Bowls, Ben, please.'

She picked up the spoon, looking thoughtfully at the empty seat beside Joanna. 'Your dad, Lauren. You'll need to fetch him.'

Before Lauren could move Joanna leapt up. 'I'll go. Don't wait.' She moved jauntily to the door and let it swing shut behind her.

Grace seemed to know exactly how much to ladle into each bowl so there was enough for everyone. Lauren watched her, memorising just how to do it in case it was her job another day.

They had only just started eating when the other two came. Lauren shot a quick look at her father as he seated himself in the chair left for him. He was smiling, and so was Joanna. As he picked up his spoon he shot a look across the table at his daughter, and raised one eyebrow. 'OK?' he mouthed at her.

Lauren made herself smile back, and nod. Of course everything was OK. Why shouldn't it be? Among this lot she was safe from being found by the brother she didn't want. And that was the reason for being here.

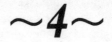

~4~

Ben must have said something to his mother because as soon as the lunch table was cleared Grace sent Lauren up to the cottage. 'To get things sorted,' she said.

Gratefully Lauren set to work. Not that there was a lot to do. In fact half an hour was plenty to arrange the contents of the chest of drawers in her room to her satisfaction. Most of it had been done last night anyway.

Downstairs in the kitchen again she cleared the ash from the grate and carried it out to the dustbin. Then she opened the packet of firelighters Grace had left handy and placed one among some wood ready for lighting later. After that she made a desultory attempt to rearrange the food cupboard, but her heart wasn't in it.

She opened the window, and leaned out to look over the lake, wondering what everyone else was doing. It was so quiet. A bird moaned in the distance, its mournful cry worse than the silence.

All of a sudden there was a tense knot of nausea inside her. What was she doing in this wild place? Home seemed a thousand miles away. She could hardly imagine what their life had been like before Mum died . . . her mother coming in from work looking pleased that tea was ready . . . wanting to know what school had been like . . . It was another world, a lying world. All pretence. And now Mum was dead, and she couldn't confront her with it and demand to know *why*.

She would give anything at this moment to be playing badminton with Vicki and going to the sports centre coffee bar afterwards. But then what . . . spending the time looking over her shoulder, afraid of someone wanting to contact her?

She took a deep, shuddering breath. The decision had been made, and it was her own decision. She had to stick it out, for Dad's sake as well as her own. He was being great about it all . . .

Banging shut the window, she grabbed up her anorak and threw it on as she left the cottage and ran down the track to the office.

Breathless, she stood for a moment outside the door. Dad had his name on it already, ARNOLD WAINWRIGHT, WARDEN in black lettering on a neat white plaque.

He looked up from a cluttered desk as she knocked and went in. The grin he gave her, though, was preoccupied, or was she only imagining it?

'I'll come back,' she said rather breathlessly, turning to fly.

'No, no, it's OK.' He pushed aside the lists he had been studying. 'Come and sit down. We need to talk.' He got up to drag forward a stool and then sat down again, clenching his fingers together in the way they used to play the finger game about churches and steeples when she was a little girl.

For a second she stared at him, too startled at the memory to say anything.

'Sit down, Lauren,' he said again, disentangling his fingers. 'I've an outline of your duties here, and your rate of pay.'

'Pay?' Lauren looked at him in surprise as she perched on the stool. She had been so intent on getting them up here to Alderdale that she hadn't given her pay any thought. Now it made her feel guilty. She leapt up. 'I haven't been doing much . . .'

'Not to panic. You're getting used to things. No one expects more of you today.' He grinned suddenly. 'Tomorrow'll be a different matter. There's this group coming, and according to Joanna we're a couple of people short this end. You'll be thrown into the deep end with a vengeance.'

Lauren smiled at him. 'That's great.'

He ran his fingers through his hair. 'It's what you need, lass. Something to do all the time. Physical exhaustion is a great help.'

He didn't have to say for what. Doing something completely new and utterly tiring would leave no time to brood for either of them.

She jumped as the phone rang, and then looked around the small office as her father picked up the receiver. On the wooden walls large-scale Ordnance Survey maps were pinned. There was a colourful poster about the Country Code, and a list of emergency phone numbers. Below the window was a long bookcase.

She got up to examine the contents, and pulled out a book on butterflies. Flipping over the pages, she looked at the bright illustrations without seeing them. Mum's face stared up at her . . . and a small two-year-old boy with sad eyes.

Her father put the phone down and got up. 'I'm needed down in the reception area immediately,' he said. 'We'll talk later. Ben could do with some assistance down in the dinghy park if you feel up to it.'

Lauren thrust the butterfly book back into place, and clattered after her father down the outside stairs.

The air was warmer now, but she shivered as she walked down the track to the lake. She would do any work that needed to be done. Dad should know that.

All the same she was taken completely by surprise. Six of the dinghies, their covers off, were parked on their trolleys on the gritty sand. Ben and Joanna, bulky in life-jackets and blue sailing anoraks, were staggering towards them carrying a huge boulder between them.

'Are you coming to help?' Joanna gasped. 'You'll need old clothes.'

Lauren gaped at the two of them. 'What on earth are you doing?'

Joanna stood upright, flexing her arms. 'Trying to sink the boats.'

Lauren looked at her suspiciously. She wasn't falling for that one.

'Buoyancy tests,' Ben said briefly, straightening up and moving towards a pile of boulders nearby.

'Tomorrow's group are keen on doing some sailing this year,' Joanna explained as she followed him. 'We've just heard, so it's all systems go to have the boats ready in time.'

'You mean, you're really serious?'

Joanna gave a gurgling laugh that was cut off in a gasp as she helped Ben pick up another boulder.

'You'll need old sailing shoes, plimsolls not trainers,' Joanna threw back over her shoulder.

'The spare ones are in the end boat,' Ben called. 'Life-jacket, too. Stick an old cagoule over your anorak. It's going to be cold. We've got to sit in the boats for half an hour.'

The cagoule Lauren found had holes in it and oil stains down the front. By the time she had donned it and the orange life-jacket the others were back with the boulder for the sixth and last boat. Hastily she slipped off her trainers and pushed her feet into the pair of sailing shoes that seemed nearest her size. Then she rolled up the legs of her jeans as the other two had done.

She was ready for anything.

With a nod to Joanna, Ben caught hold of the trolley handle and pulled it and the boat into the water. Then, ankle deep, he turned the whole lot round and gently eased the boat off the trolley. Joanna, wading in after him, took it from him. As she pulled it up, away from the water's edge to park it she shot a look of triumph at Lauren. 'Your turn next. D'you think you can manage?'

Lauren bit her lip as she watched her climb into the boat, grab a bucket from beneath the seat and begin to fill the boat with water.

It was hard not to gape. Ben gave the boat a push out into deeper water and waded back to shore. He grinned at her. 'We have to do these buoyancy tests to prove the boats will still float when full of water. It's the safety rules. We haven't enough spare bodies for two to a boat. That's why we're using the rocks.'

Put like that it made sense, but Lauren threw Ben a sideways look as he indicated the boat he wanted her to get into.

'The bucket's under the thwart, and the paddle's there too,' Ben said as he gave her a shove off. 'Fill up to gunwale level.'

The gunwale was the rim that ran all round the boat,

Lauren found as she watched Joanna. She was glad she hadn't asked about that or about what the paddle was. It was obvious.

'Coping all right, Lauren?' Ben called across to her as he climbed into his boat and pushed away from the shore with the paddle.

She nodded, surprised how tired she felt. But not cold, even though her legs were in the water.

Joanna moved alongside. 'Bet you didn't think you'd have to do yucky things like this, Lauren. But this is only the start of it. Isn't that right, Ben?'

Ben nodded as he continued flooding his boat with rhythmic scoops of his bucket. Lauren glanced at him, thinking how different he seemed from the shy boy yesterday. Today he was in charge, and it showed in the confident way he had held himself when explaining things to her. And Joanna seemed to think he knew what he was doing, too.

'What made you and your dad apply for the job here, Lauren?' Joanna asked, her eyes gleaming. 'Go on, tell!'

'We wanted a change of scene.' Lauren's face felt stiff, and she didn't look at Joanna. It was true, wasn't it, so why did she feel so guilty? She wished Joanna would leave her alone, but knew she wouldn't.

'It's quiet here for a girl like you, miles from anywhere.'

Lauren didn't reply. With her head turned away she watched as Ben moved his boat sluggishly towards them.

'Managing all right?' he called across to her. 'Bet you didn't imagine yourself doing anything as mad as this!'

It was more or less what Joanna had said, but it didn't sound like an interrogation this time. Lauren tried to think of intelligent questions to ask him to prevent any more from Joanna, but Joanna wasn't going to let up.

'Your dad,' she said, her voice husky. 'What did he do before . . . the same sort of thing? We've been trying to get a new warden for ages and then suddenly here he is. I smell mystery.' She laughed again, obviously enjoying herself.

'Have you been here long?' Lauren asked Ben, her voice desperate.

He threw her a sympathetic look, and she concentrated hard on what he told her about his mum taking on the job as catering organiser when his dad died. 'There's plenty doing between Easter and September,' he said. 'You'll like it when the group comes tomorrow.'

She wanted to ask him what he did during the winter months, but there was no chance with Joanna's husky comments all the time.

'You're a lucky girl having a dad like yours,' Joanna said, holding her paddle in her hands, ready to move nearer. 'Are you the only one? Your mum died, didn't she?'

'Mum died,' Lauren said through dry lips. And just shut up, she wanted to add.

Instead she thrust her paddle overboard and moved away. Behind her she heard Ben's voice asking Joanna about something or other. She couldn't hear what, for the angry buzzing in her ears.

By the time they were finished and emptying the water out of the last boat she was exhausted.

She dragged herself up to the cottage to shower and change, glad there was no evening meal to prepare. Grace had all that under control in the clubhouse kitchen.

'I've been looking after your little girl, Arnold,' Joanna said playfully as they all sat down and began to eat. She had a triumphant gleam in her eyes as she looked at him.

Cringing inside, Lauren helped herself to a wholemeal

roll. Dad smiled across at her, looking as pleased as if he'd won the pools. Surely he wasn't going to fall for that sort of talk? She threw him an indignant look, but he didn't notice. He was too busy passing things to Joanna and grinning at every stupid remark she made.

Afterwards Grace insisted that she rest. 'You've done wonders today, Lauren,' she said. 'Why don't you get an early night?'

Ben gave a great yawn which he tried to smother with a cough. Only Joanna seemed perfectly fresh . . . and that was exactly the right word, Lauren thought dismally as she got up from the table.

It was cold in the cottage. She reached for the matches Grace had left for them and knelt in front of the fire to light it. There was something comforting in watching the flames lick the wood and start to take hold. By the time her father pushed open the door and came into the kitchen the warmth was like a comfortable shield.

'By!' he said, rubbing his hands. 'That looks good.'

She smiled up at him. 'Come and sit down, Dad. Coffee?'

He shook his head as he came to stand with his back to the fire. 'Joanna made me one. So . . . have you had a good day?'

She nodded. 'Great. Except that Joanna kept asking questions about why we came here.'

'Joanna?' He moved his weight from one foot to the other and gazed down at her, frowning. 'Joanna's being friendly, that's all.'

She saw the lines of tiredness round his eyes. He had worked hard, too, and for the same reason as herself.

Impulsively she sprang up, and threw her arms round his neck. 'Do you like it here, Dad? We won't stay if you don't.'

He gave a deep rumbling laugh as he held her in a tight hug for a second, and then let her go. 'Get off to bed, lass, and don't talk nonsense. It's good for both of us, having so much to occupy us. No time to brood about the past, eh?'

She stood silent, thinking of Joanna's probing questions which had brought everything back so vividly when she wanted to forget. Tomorrow she must avoid her . . . but could she? It was all right for Dad. He could shut himself away in his office for hours at a time.

But Dad didn't want to avoid Joanna, or so it seemed. She gave a weak smile, and looked at him as if he was a stranger.

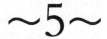

~5~

Lauren was pleased to see that nearly everyone in the hiking group was wearing trainers like herself. Only Richard, one of the leaders of the church group from Misterdale, stout and rosy-faced, was kitted out in boots and thick socks over his cords. He wore a huge orange cagoule and a red knitted hat that looked as if it had seen combat. One of the others wore a woolly hat, too, a light grey one that matched the colour of his eyes. A lock of straight fair hair stuck out at the front.

It was so much better now the group had come. For one thing Joanna was fully occupied, as they all were. From the moment the coach had come lumbering down the track and emptied its human cargo it had been all go.

Now the tents were up, the group split into three and she had been delegated to accompany the hikers.

Richard waited until they had all set off up the hillside before striding through them to reach Lauren's side.

'Done anything like this before?' he asked her. His

eyes seemed to vanish into the folds of flesh as he smiled. He exuded warmth and vitality, and she found herself walking faster because of it.

'Not for a long time. Dad used to take us for long walks when we stayed with my grandfather in Cornwall.'

'An easy walk today,' Richard said, smiling at her with confidence. 'You'll be all right. Get to know the lie of the land a bit.'

It didn't seem easy as they left the track and set off in single file up an almost non-existent path. Richard, immediately in front of her, looked round every now and again to check they were all following. The fair-haired boy in the grey woolly hat was behind her, carrying a map in a plastic case.

The air was like honey . . . fresh and sweet-smelling at the same time. She could smell the earth, too, as her legs swished through the bracken. The sense of space and timelessness was exhilarating.

At last Richard stopped on the brow of the hill. 'Come on then, Tom,' he said in his booming voice. 'You're the map-reader.'

The grey-hatted boy leapt off the tuffet of thick grass on which he stood poised, and grinned at Richard. A few of the others crowded round, and he looked over their heads at Lauren. 'Want a look? See, we're here, and that's what we're making for.' He held the map up high so she could see.

After that she found he was often at her side, explaining things and pointing the misty shape of Greater Whernside rising above the distant hills. There was a grouse, too, that shot out of the heather ahead of them, which she would never have recognised on her own.

She thought suddenly of the butterfly book she was

looking at yesterday, and of Mum's face that had seemed to look up at her from the page. Quickly she banished it, and concentrated hard on keeping up with the rest as they sprang down the hill to the roadside.

To her surprise the Adventure Centre van drew up and Grace opened the door and got out. She smiled at Lauren, her face losing the pucker of lines between her eyes for a moment.

Lauren was glad to see her, and it wasn't only because Grace had brought the food and drink for their lunch. She was a welcome link with the familiar.

Tom came to sit beside Lauren. He pulled off his hat and she saw that his hair was long and slightly wavy at the back. Rubbing his hand across his warm forehead he began to talk to her about the engineering course he was doing at college in Newcastle.

He bit deeply into a ham roll, his grey eyes shining in an enthusiasm that was infectious. 'I help out with this church youth group sometimes at weekends,' he said. 'I've got to get back home tonight, though. It's my grandparents' Golden Wedding tomorrow and they'll have my guts for garters if I'm not there.' He laughed as he reached for two cans of Coke and passed one to Lauren. 'You know what families are like. Mine are worse than most. Kept chained hand and foot I am.'

Lauren laughed too. 'So how come you're here now?'

'I escaped, didn't I?'

'If I believed that I'd believe anything.'

He flipped his can open and tilted his head back to drink. She couldn't imagine anyone less downtrodden. He gave the impression of doing exactly what he thought was right, and woe to anyone who stood in his way. He was fond of his grandparents. You could see that by the way he'd smiled when he mentioned them.

She opened her can too. 'So, how are you getting home?'

'No problem. Richard'll give me a lift down to Rawthwaite and then I'll hitch to Harrogate and get a train.'

'At that time of night?'

'Sure. I'll sleep on the train if I have to.'

'But won't they worry about you?'

He wiped the back of his hand across his mouth, and then crushed his empty can between his fingers and put it in his rucksack. 'Don't know I'm coming, do they? It's a surprise.'

'But you said they'd have your guts for garters if you weren't there.'

'Persistent, aren't you? Where d'you get it from . . . your dad?'

Lauren frowned. 'What's Dad got to do with it?'

He laughed, and sprang up. 'Ah well, just testing, that's all.'

He moved off to talk to someone else. Seeing she was on her own, Richard came to sit down beside her, puffing a little. He had finished his own lunch. He undid his rucksack, and got out a small, worn-looking book that she saw to her surprise was a New Testament.

He smiled as he saw her looking at it, and smoothed the cover with his plump fingers. 'This is my companion everywhere I go. I was just making sure it was here, my memory being what it is. Yours is in fine fettle, being young, but us oldies have to help ours along a bit.'

Lauren gave a little sigh. 'My memory's too good sometimes. I wish . . .'

He raised one eyebrow at her, which gave his chubby face a comical look, but he didn't say anything. She picked a blade of grass and looked at it speculatively.

She had never met anyone like Richard before. Even though he was short and overweight there was a sort of dignity about him that she liked. She hardly knew him, but it seemed as if she had known him always. Perhaps it was the way he had of not asking even the most elementary questions she might have expected from someone who was in charge of this group and hadn't met her before. All he had talked about was hiking, and she had told him about the walks they used to do when she was small, she and Dad and Mum.

She raised the grass to her lips and started to chew the end, savouring the sweetness of the white stem. With her eyes on the distant fells she began to enlarge on some of their walks, remembering them as clearly as if they had happened yesterday.

'Mum used to like walking,' she said, dreamily. Suddenly she remembered her grandfather's Bible and the way he had read something out to her one day when they got back from a walk about flowers blooming in the desert. Her forehead creased into lines of concentration.

It had been too windy for the beach so Dad had taken them up on Bodmin Moor. The wind had nearly blown them over up there, and they had laughed as they leaned into it. For once the ground wasn't soggy as they walked across from the car to the outcrop of grey rock on the summit of a small tor. The dusty earth had dulled her new trainers, and all she could think about at the time was how she'd only bought them the day before in Newquay.

With startling clarity she remembered just how it had been – Mum laughing as she told grandad about it when they got back to his house, and the words he quoted.

'The wilderness and the solitary place shall be glad for them; and the desert shall rejoice, and blossom as the rose', Lauren murmured now. 'It shall blossom abundantly . . .'

'and rejoice even with joy and singing', Richard finished for her.

She sat upright, brushing the quick tears from her eyes. 'How did you know that?'

'It's Isaiah, in the Old Testament. I can't remember the exact chapter and verse, but it's a lovely piece. I can't look the rest up for you in here, of course, but it's crammed with lovely passages.'

She looked at his New Testament, held lovingly in his hand.

There were signs of movement now with everyone getting up, and Grace collecting the bits and pieces to carry back to the van.

There was more climbing to do as they set off again. On the brow of a higher hill the wind caught them, ruffling Lauren's hair, and she could see the reason for the woolly hats. Tom's was stuffed in his pocket though, part of it hanging out.

'Mind you don't lose it,' she said to him.

He pulled it out, and stuck it on the top of his head, and she found herself laughing with him as they all set off again in single file.

'That's the new reservoir,' Tom said, serious now as they ambled down towards a sheet of water. 'The last time we came they were excavating. You can't imagine the mess. It looks so different now.'

They all stopped again to gaze. Tom stood on an outcrop of rock, his grey-hatted head silhouetted against the calm water. In the distance the bleat of a sheep sounded like a kitten's mew.

Lauren took a deep breath, and let it out slowly. It was so different, so strange. Like another world. And suddenly, she liked it. She liked the fresh wind on her face, and the feeling of isolation. Even the dragging exhaustion in her limbs was pleasant because it stopped her thinking of anything else except the wish to keep up with the rest and to last out the course.

She and Tom fell a little behind once they'd left the reservoir behind them. They trudged in silence until they reached another track that seemed to wind round the hillside for ever.

'How much further?' she asked.

For answer he produced his map. 'See here,' he said, pointing to an area of thick contours. 'Up this path here, and round here, and down through a gorge there and up a peak here . . .'

She craned forward to look. 'So where's the reservoir we passed? We can't have that far to go.'

'Reservoir . . . what reservoir?' He looked at her in mock surprise.

She smiled. 'You're having me on again.'

'Just testing,' he said as he got up and slung the map in its plastic case inside his anorak. 'Quick off the mark, aren't you? Go to the top of the class.'

Even though Lauren's face felt red and her hair straggled into her neck she didn't want the hike to end. There was a happiness in it that shut out everything else. For a little while at least she had forgotten why she was here in Alderdale.

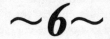

~6~

Lauren threw herself down on the grass in front of the clubhouse. Immediately Tom ripped off his trainers, and the others did the same.

The relief of it! Lauren wriggled her toes, smiling slightly.

But they weren't allowed to rest for long. Richard came striding up to them, his rucksack slung over one arm, and his orange cagoule in the other. 'Everyone back to the tents to change. The meal's ready and we're late.'

There wasn't time to return to the cottage. Lauren put her trainers back on, and took off her anorak. She tried to straighten her hair as she went up the steps into the clubhouse.

Joanna was there already, cool and relaxed, her dark hair shining. 'So,' she drawled as she saw Lauren, 'the wanderer returns. A good day out, was it? All right for some!'

Lauren's face was warm from her exertions, but she felt her flush deepen. She had accompanied the hikers on

Ben's instructions and not because she wanted an easy time of it. She glared.

Joanna, not a bit disconcerted, smiled back as the others came pouring in. It was easy to see that she'd positioned herself opposite the door deliberately.

When Dad came in, though, he didn't make for the empty seat on the other side of Joanna, but took one down at the other end. He was frowning, his dark eyebrows pulled close together. At some remark from Tom he gave a laugh that didn't quite reach his eyes.

Lauren looked at him as the plates were collected after the main course. His preoccupied expression meant he had something on his mind. Not Joanna, surely?

She glanced at her and surprised a hard look on the older woman's face. It was clear that the empty seat at her side was a challenge. Joanna said nothing, though, until the meal was finished.

'Did you tell Arnold you'd damaged one of the boats, Ben?' she called to him.

Ben flushed. 'I haven't had a chance yet.'

Joanna raised her eyebrows. 'No? Then we'd better talk about it now, hadn't we?' She raised her voice. 'Want to hear the details, Arnold, or are you too busy?'

He got up from his place to move next to Joanna. Tom gave a low whistle. 'So that's how it's done,' he said quietly.

Lauren scowled as she began to pile up the dishes.

'Don't let the wind change when you're looking like that,' Tom said in a mock-serious voice before giving a loud laugh.

Lauren laughed too, and felt herself relax.

The group had more activities planned for them, and were soon off. Of those remaining, only Joanna and her father were still seated at the table, with Ben at their side.

'Joanna's making too much of it,' Grace's calm voice said as Lauren helped carry plates into the kitchen. 'Ben will sort out the repairs quite easily if she leaves him to it. Why not go down to the boatyard with him and see the damage, Lauren? You're excused duties here. It'll get him away from Joanna.'

Ben seemed relieved as they went down the steps and across the grass. He didn't say anything though. Tom would have joked and clowned, but not Ben. He walked silently at her side, his eyes on the lake ahead of them. It was strange the way she felt she knew all these people so well when this time last week she hadn't known that any of them existed.

A gash the size of a five pound note dented the side of the boat Lauren recognized as one she had used for the buoyancy test. From Joanna's description she had expected the whole of the side to be caved in.

Ben bent to examine it, running his hand across it experimentally. He didn't look as if he was still smarting about Joanna's attack, but Lauren wasn't sure.

It's my dad she's after, not you, she wanted to say. But how could she, without getting in far too deeply for her peace of mind?

Ben straightened. 'It's not too bad. I'll get working on it in the morning and patch it up. Someone got a bit too near my boat, that's all, and couldn't go about in time.'

'So it wasn't your fault?'

He shrugged. 'I was in charge. It was my responsibility.'

'So why didn't you tell Joanna it wasn't your fault?'

'She knew that already.'

'And you let her get away with it?'

He shrugged again. 'She wanted to get a rise out of me, that's all. I always play her at her own game, and take no notice.'

Lauren was indignant. 'Game? It doesn't seem much of a game to me.'

He gave her a quizzical look, and then his slow smile reached his eyes. 'It's the best way of getting at Joanna, you'll see.'

Lauren smiled too, though she wasn't entirely convinced.

In silence they walked up the track. As they reached the tents she saw the group seated in a circle. There was no sign of Tom.

She turned accusingly to Ben. 'Tom's gone home and I didn't say goodbye!'

Richard gave her a wave to attract her attention. 'Your Dad's taken Tom down to Rawthwaite,' he bellowed. 'He'll not be long.'

She felt let down. Tom had helped to make the day good for her. 'I ought to have said goodbye,' she said, glaring at Ben as if it was all his fault.

Ben said nothing. There wasn't much to say anyway, but his lips had tightened and he didn't look at her.

She moved towards Richard whose eyes crinkled as he smiled at her. 'There's coffee for us all in the clubhouse,' he said. 'Coming?'

They sat on the balcony, looking out over the peaceful lake. As she sipped her coffee Lauren listened to Richard's deep voice talking about the lovely verses in the Bible that they had quoted earlier. For a moment her mother seemed very near because they were the verses that she had liked too.

Richard moved slightly in his chair at last as he placed his empty coffee mug on a nearby table. 'I thought afterwards that I should have given you this.'

To her surprise he took his New Testament out of his

pocket, and leaned forward to place it in her lap.

'But it's yours,' she said. 'You'll miss having it in your rucksack. How will you manage without it?'

He smiled. 'If you have it, I'll have it too.'

She didn't understand what he meant, but she knew she couldn't refuse to take it. 'Thank you, Richard. I'll take care of it.'

He scraped his chair back as he got up to take the mugs back to the kitchen. Lauren put his New Testament into her pocket, but kept her hand on it in case it should slip out.

Much later, showered and in her pyjamas, Lauren leaned back in the big armchair and opened Richard's New Testament. The book opened at Matthew chapter seven as if he had often read those verses himself. Perhaps he knew them by heart. He'd quoted that bit out of Isaiah as if he was familiar with it, but he couldn't know the whole Bible off by heart, surely, or why bother to carry this little book about with him in his rucksack? Anyway he wouldn't be carrying it now because he had given it to her.

She smiled, remembering the warmth Richard's quotation had generated in her. It was like a light shining inside her. She looked down at the words in front of her. 'Ask, and you will receive;' she read, 'seek, and you will find; knock, and the door will be opened to you. For everyone who asks will receive, and anyone who seeks will find, and the door will be opened to him who knocks.'

It was a definite promise, wasn't it? 'Ask, and you will receive.' So if she asked she would receive. If she asked to be allowed to get on with her life here in peace with herself then her prayer would be answered. That's what it said here clearly in black and white. 'Please God,' she begged. 'Please . . . let me forget. Please don't let him come here when I don't want him to . . . help us to get on with our lives . . .'

She was almost asleep with fatigue and fresh air by the time the cottage door opened. She struggled to sit up, and stared at her father as he came slowly into the room.

'You've been ages,' she accused. 'I didn't know where you'd got to.'

He gave a tired smile. 'I could use a coffee.'

She got up to make one for him and for herself. She yawned, relieved he was here at last but wondering at the same time why taking Tom down to Rawthwaite had taken him so long.

He sat in the chair with his hands hanging down at his side as if he was too exhausted to do anything about them. She placed his coffee beside him.

'I ran the young lad right into Harrogate,' he said at last. 'Got a lot to say for himself, hasn't he? He's a great help to the Misterdale group by all accounts.'

She nodded. 'So that's why you took a long time.'

He reached for his mug of coffee and sat with his hands wrapped round it. 'That, and sitting in the car at the top of the lane for a bit.'

'Alone?' Her tone was too sharp, and she coughed to cover it.

He nodded as he put the mug back on the table. 'The lake looked stunning with the afterglow on it. The hills behind had this lovely pink sheen. This is a beautiful place, lass. You like it here? You've had a good day?'

She smiled, and yawned wide again. 'A great day, Dad. You've no need to worry about me.'

His face softened. He stood up, and ruffled her hair. 'Bed now, I think.'

'Your coffee. You haven't drunk it.'

He looked at it as if wondering how it got there. She was so tired it didn't occur to her until afterwards to wonder why he had felt it necessary to sit alone in the car at the top of the lane when he must have known she would be wondering where he was.

To her surprise Lauren woke early next morning. It wasn't until a couple of days later that the hikes she'd been doing in the fresh moorland air began to catch up with her and she slept late. The sun was slanting in through the living-room window by the time she went in for breakfast.

She didn't see the note propped against the marmalade jar until she had made a pot of tea. 'Had to get down to the office early today,' he'd written in his big sprawling handwriting. 'No rush for you to get going. Ben said last night that there's a late start for you people today. See you later. Dad.'

She gave a little shrug as she began to eat. Today the Misterdalers were going off by coach on a day trip and Joanna was going with them. Ben hadn't told her what he wanted her to do, but Dad was right about not needing to rush.

The postman came as she was washing up. Drying her hands, she went to the door to greet him and take the post. She glanced at it as she shut the door behind him. It was all for the Centre except an official-looking letter addressed to Dad with Jones and Bateson, Solicitors, 3 Abson Street, York, North Yorkshire emblazoned in thick black lettering at the top of the envelope. It had PRIVATE AND CONFIDENTIAL on it too.

Lauren dropped the letter on top of the others as if it was red-hot. She stared at it, her mouth dry, knowing it was connected with the very thing she and Dad had come to Alderdale to forget. So, her desperate prayer the other evening had been too late.

Then, suddenly, she grabbed up the pile of letters and ran out of the cottage. By the time she reached the steps to the office she was gasping and had to stand still for a moment with her hand on the rail to get her breath back.

The office was empty. She stared in disbelief. It was vital she see Dad at once, so where was he? She sprang round as she heard light footsteps behind her and saw Grace in the doorway.

'Your dad's downstairs somewhere,' Grace said, smiling. 'Is that the mail?'

Lauren held it out to her and watched while she sifted through and then put them in a neat pile in the in-tray left ready for the purpose. The solicitor's letter was still on top, but Grace seemed to think it of no particular importance. And why should she? It was causing such blood-chilling apprehension only to herself.

Lauren's heart felt heavy as they went downstairs again. At the bottom Grace turned to her. 'Ben would like your help laying the orienteering course this morning, Lauren. Has he said anything . . . no? Find your dad first if you want. Ben'll wait.'

Her father was nowhere to be seen. It wasn't until Ben appeared that she discovered that Dad had found it necessary to visit the bank down in Rawthwaite, and wouldn't be around for a while.

'Is it important?' Ben asked as he smoothed his dark hair off his forehead. He looked ready for action in his jeans and navy sweatshirt. She was so used to seeing him in shorts that he looked taller today.

Lauren shifted her feet. 'Yes . . . well, no. I don't know. It will have to wait then.'

He looked at her anxiously as he humped his rucksack

over one shoulder. 'Are you all right? You don't look it. It's OK. I can manage on my own.'

Lauren took a deep, calming breath. 'Orienteering, your Mum said. What do we have to do?'

Ben looked at her quickly. 'Right then. It means a lot of tramping about, putting down the numbers and the clues. Any good at map references?'

She had done something about it at school, but having Ben explain about it as they set off was far more interesting. She was reminded of Tom larking about on the hillside with his map the other day and pretending they had much farther to go than they really had.

Every now and again Ben produced cards wrapped in polythene, to be fixed at certain points on the hillside above the clubhouse.

'I wonder when Tom will be coming back?' she said, almost to herself.

Ben looked surprised. 'Who?'

'He went back for his grandparents' Golden Wedding. You know . . . Tom. The one helping Richard with the Misterdalers.'

'Oh, him.' Ben looked as if he didn't want to talk about Tom. He turned his head and looked over towards the group of hills on the skyline.

As they reached the top of the hill Lauren kept looking back as if she expected her father to appear from nowhere.

'Tom won't come back here today anyway,' Ben said, stopping to rub his hand across his warm forehead. His eyes looked troubled.

'It's Dad,' Lauren said quickly. 'I've got to see him.'

Ben shrugged. 'Women! I told you he'd gone to the bank.'

He had, of course. He must think her crazy.

The sun was warm on her back as they trudged up through the heather; down below, the lake sparkled gold and silver. Once over the brow of the hill the countryside changed, and she could see fields edged with stone walls, and a few trees grouped together as if for company. She gazed at them, miles away in thought and seeing only the unopened letter on Dad's desk. Suppose . . .

'Watch it!' Ben cried. 'What's the matter with you?'

She came to, startled, in time to avoid the large hole in the path in front of her. She saw then that the ground was dropping away steeply on the part of hillside they were on, and she must take care. 'Sorry,' she muttered as she followed him down the narrow path to the trees at the bottom. She watched him tie a card to a low hanging branch and then pull some ivy across to hide it.

He smiled in satisfaction. 'They won't find that one in a hurry.'

She looked vague. 'Find what?'

He dumped his rucksack on the ground. 'You really are in a state, aren't you?'

She looked at him without speaking for a moment while he found an outcrop of rock for a seat. If only she could talk about the letter. She needed Vicki here . . . someone who understood how it had been when Uncle Dave had told them about Mum.

'Did Dad say how long he'd be?' she said at last.

He patted the rock at his side. 'Come and have a sit down, for goodness sake. How should I know? He'll be back by lunchtime, I expect.'

She collapsed on the rock at his side with her legs stretched out in front of her, willing the time to pass quickly so she could get back and find out what was going on.

'I wonder how the others are getting on?' Ben said.

'Have you ever been to York?'

She sat bolt upright. '*York?*'

'They're going to the Jorvik Viking Centre first, you know, going back into the past and seeing it all as if it's real. Even the talking and the smells . . . why, what's wrong, Lauren?'

She was staring at him, white-faced, still shocked at his mention of York. York . . . where the letter came from. But Ben couldn't know that, or why she didn't want to think about York. She gave a little gasp, and tried to smile.

Ben glanced at her anxiously, then busied himself sorting the remaining cards. 'Not many more to do now. Do you want to stay here while I get the rest in position?'

For answer she sprang up, trying to put the letter out of her mind. She smiled. 'Can I see the map?'

He passed it to her. She knew that he had planned the route before they set out to place the clues. All she had to do was hold the cards and make sure the right numbers were attached in the correct places. Simple. Too simple, though, to engage her mind fully. She made a determined effort to imagine how hard the participants were going to find the clues Ben had thought up.

'When are they going to do this orienteering?' she asked as they set off again.

Ben held a branch back for her so that it didn't spring back and hit her in the face. 'Tomorrow, I think. That's why the cards are wrapped in plastic. No good if they get wet.'

She imagined the frustration of not being able to read the clues properly, and then tried to think of more questions to ask to show Ben she was really interested.

She must have succeeded because he no longer looked anxious as they returned to the Adventure Centre at last.

~7~

Grace had their lunch ready – soup and rolls followed by yoghurt.

Lauren looked at it in dismay as she seated herself at the table. Food would choke her, she knew it would. If only Dad would come . . .

She heard him come in before the others were aware that he had returned. But even then she had to wait in silence while he greeted Grace and Ben and then sat down to eat his lunch with evident enjoyment.

'Lauren was looking for you,' she heard Grace say.

He cocked an eyebrow at her, helping himself to another roll.

'There's a letter,' she said quietly. Of course he hadn't been up to the office yet. He hadn't seen the letter, but he seemed to sense there was something more important than usual waiting for him upstairs. He got up, wiping his mouth. 'Let's go and see then. OK?'

He slit the envelope with his pocket knife, and then sat reading it with an anxious frown creasing his brows.

He looked up at last. 'Sit down, Lauren, and listen. It's from a solicitor in York.'

'And?' Lauren sat down with a thump. 'What does he want?'

'His client is Stephen Thomas Harmer . . . your half-brother. He's been instructed to enquire if a meeting between the two of you can be arranged in the near future.'

Lauren stared wide-eyed at her father, her mouth dry.

'What will you say to him?' she whispered at last.

Her father looked at her over the top of the letter. 'Say? It's not for me to say, lass. It's your decision. OK?'

She nodded, opening her mouth to speak and then shutting it again. Her sense of loss was so sharp she was unable to speak for a moment. She had known all along that something like this would happen. He'd been a shadowy figure up to now, but this letter immediately turned her half-brother into someone real and menacing. Stephen Harmer, she thought frantically. Real flesh and blood and wanting to meet her . . .

'How did he know?' she cried. 'Who told him where to find us?'

Her father looked as puzzled as she was herself as he folded the letter, thought better of it and then opened it out on the desk in front of him again.

Lauren shivered. 'Uncle Dave must have . . . but he only knows our home address so it couldn't have been Uncle Dave.'

'It's done. Whoever it was it makes no difference.'

'I don't like it, writing to us here.'

'It's happened, OK? Don't dwell on it, just tell me what you want me to do.'

She bit her lip. There was no decision to make really. Dad knew what she would say. She clenched her hands together in her lap. 'I won't meet him. He's no right to make me.'

Her father was strangely silent.

'Dad, you don't think . . . you can't . . . ?'

He shook his head. 'I want you to be sure, Lauren, that's all. The chance won't come again. You don't want any regrets.'

'Never!'

Arnold Wainwright drew his brows together, and looked at his daughter with a grave expression in his eyes. Then he folded the letter again and replaced it in its envelope. 'I'll get something off to the solicitor right away then. But you're absolutely sure about this?'

'Quite sure,' she said vehemently. Of course she was sure, dead sure. She would have nothing to do with this Stephen Harmer . . . ever.

'Think of the boy's side of it, though. He feels strongly about it or he wouldn't have taken it this far. Think on it.'

'Whose side are you on, Dad, his or mine?'

His hurt look was almost more than she could bear. 'Oh Dad, I didn't mean it!'

'I know, lass, I know. There's no more to be said. The matter's closed. Agreed?'

She tried to smile. 'Agreed.'

'That's my Lauren. Know your own mind, and have no regrets.'

'No regrets,' she promised him as she stood up. 'But Dad . . . suppose he takes no notice and comes here anyway?'

'If he'd do that he wouldn't have bothered with asking through a solicitor. Nay, he'll not bother you when he gets our reply. Don't worry about it.'

Lauren could feel only relief now. The worst had happened, and she could make her feelings clear through Dad.

She thought suddenly of Richard's New Testament, felt in her pocket for it and then remembered she'd left it on her bed. 'Ask, and you will receive,' she thought. She *had* asked, hadn't she? There was no need to worry any more. Because of the letter, she had been given the opportunity to make her feelings about meeting her half-brother crystal clear.

Suddenly she became aware of such surrounding peace that she gazed at her father in wonder.

He looked as if he had all the cares of the world on his shoulders. 'It's all right, Dad,' she said quickly. 'Everything's going to be all right.' She caught hold of his hand and squeezed it. 'Get involved with your work now,' she advised. 'It's the best way.' This was more or less what he had told her to do and now here she was repeating it.

As Lauren left the office and ran down the stairs she saw Ben standing on the grass with his head thrown back and a finger held high in the air. 'Practically no wind at the moment,' he said when he saw her.

'What *are* you doing?' she asked in surprise.

'Testing for wind direction, of course.' He licked his finger, and held it up again. 'Just a breath of breeze at the moment, but it may get up. Fancy a sail, Lauren? It's a good chance for me to put you in the picture a bit.'

He sounded as if he thought she might refuse, but she needed no second invitation.

To her surprise she saw that the repairs had been started already on the damaged boat. 'It didn't take you long to get working on it then?'

Ben ripped apart the Velcro fastening on the nylon cover of the boat parked next to it. 'The primer has to dry before I can do any more.'

She looked at it in wonder. 'You must have been up very early this morning.'

He nodded. 'It had to be done. Stick the cover over there while I get the sails out.'

By the time Ben had shown her how to rig the boat, Lauren felt a flicker of breeze on her cheek.

'Wind's coming,' he said in satisfaction. He had his shorts on under his jeans which he removed now. He pulled his life-jacket on over his sweatshirt but left it hanging open.

She helped him get the boat on its trolley down to the water's edge and waited until she could help pull up the mainsail. Then she rolled the legs of her jeans up as high as they would go and fastened her life-jacket before taking the empty trolley from him to park on the grass.

This time the boat was high in the water as she clambered in. Ben fixed the rudder and tiller and they were off. She was surprised at the amount of wind now.

'Centreboard down,' Ben said sharply. 'Here . . . like this.' He leaned forward so far to show her she thought he would fall over her and the boat tip over.

She bit back a gasp.

He grinned as he moved back. 'All right?'

'All right,' she said, meaning it. It was great. They zoomed across the lake with the far bank coming at them fast. She didn't know how they would turn, but there was something about the competent way Ben was handling the boat that made her trust him completely.

Quickly he explained about her changing sides and pulling the jib sheet through when he gave the command. Then it was 'Ready about? Lee-ho,' and they were round and sailing diagonally back across the lake.

Back and forth they went, and each time they changed

direction Lauren felt more confident. She was able to look around a bit now. The clubhouse and the tents in front of it looked different from the water, more compact somehow and small against the background of hills.

Her face glowed as a spray of lake water splattered her.

'You're a natural,' Ben said. 'You'll be taking a boat out on your own soon!'

She laughed, delighting in the rising wind that filled the sails so satisfactorily. It was hard to think of problems and worries with the spray breaking over you and your hair almost skimming the water as the boat tilted.

They were near the head of the lake now, and she didn't want to go back.

'Ready about? Lee-ho,' Ben called, and they were round. Now the sails were well out on either side of the boat and the wind seemed still. It couldn't be, of course, with the sails out like balloons.

'We're running,' Ben explained as he moved the tiller out slightly. 'The wind's behind us now. Bring the centreboard up a bit.'

She knew what to do. As she glanced back over the stern she could see by their wake that they were moving faster than she had thought. She turned to smile at Ben, and saw an answering gleam in his eyes. It felt great being part of a team, the two of them. He seemed to think so, too.

But now that they were moving smoothly with the wind behind them the thought of the solicitor's letter came rushing back.

'Have you ever had a big decision to make, Ben? One that really mattered?' she asked.

He looked thoughtful, leaning back a little. 'A really big one? Well . . . not really. Only like backing Mum when she wanted to come here. But that wasn't my decision really, though I approved. I knew it was right for us.'

Lauren moved her position slightly, and stared overboard at the lake water flowing past. 'I had to make a big one just now.'

He didn't ask any questions. In fact he didn't say anything. She didn't either, for a few minutes.

'I had to make it the way I did,' she said at last as if he knew all about it and didn't need telling. She sat up straight. Somehow voicing her thoughts out loud was helping her to come to terms with the letter. It had to be as Dad said . . . who would bother getting a solicitor to write if he intended to show up anyway?

Now it was time to go about again, and Ben was busy explaining what was happening. Backwards and forwards they went until at last Ben glanced at his watch. 'Had enough yet, Lauren? Time to go in.'

She smiled, and moved her hair out of her eyes with her free hand. The other was holding on to the jib sheet and pulling it in tightly as he instructed. The boat was tilted well over and she knew she had to keep the small sail tight. 'Must we?'

''Fraid so.'

They couldn't stay out here on the lake for ever, but that's what she felt like doing. It wasn't only peace she felt surrounding her now, but something else too, a feeling of being cared for in a way she hadn't experienced before, not even from Dad. Maybe the fresh moorland air on her face had something to do with it, and the feeling of space and light and freedom that sailing gave her. Whatever it was she wanted more of it, and it was frustrating to have to go back to shore.

'You really like this, Lauren, don't you?' Ben was

looking at her with a glow about him that made him seem older. She saw that his eyes gleamed in his tanned face. He looked as if he didn't want this moment to end, either.

It seemed no time at all until they were nearing the boatyard again and he was explaining that she should read the books he'd lend her about the different points of sailing.

'Oh, I will,' she said as she swung her legs over the side and waded ashore to retrieve the trolley.

Up on the slipway they removed the sails in companionable silence. As Ben placed the rudder and tiller tidily on one of the thwarts, though, he mentioned having another sailing lesson very soon. 'If you can help with the sailing, Lauren, it'll free Joanna.'

She gazed at him, serious-eyed. She could feel the warmth in the atmosphere fade. 'Free Joanna for what?'

He gave a quick, surprised look, and then busied himself with folding the sails and stuffing them in the sail bag. 'Leading the other activities, of course. What do you think?'

The Misterdale group wouldn't be back till late afternoon, and Ben had work to do on the boat. Lauren felt a shaft of loneliness as she went up to the clubhouse to help Grace prepare for the evening meal.

It was peaceful in the kitchen, chopping up vegetables for the casserole.

'The sailing was fine,' Lauren said as she worked, 'specially when the wind got up and we had to sit right out.'

'You weren't worried?'

Lauren shook her head. 'The fast bits were best. Ben's a good sailor.'

Grace smiled, looking pleased. 'He teaches sailing well.

Always has done. He got his R.Y.A. certificate early and he's well qualified.'

Lauren reached for more carrots to peel and slice. She worked fast, moving the knife deftly. 'Where did he learn?'

'He taught himself really. We lived near the sea at Redcar after his father died. Then we moved to the Dales before coming here three years ago.'

'You came here three years ago? I thought it was longer than that.'

'We came when the Adventure Centre was set up. It seemed like an answer to prayer. Ben was alone so much. Maybe that's what made him into a loner.' She gave a little sigh. 'He was at school then, of course, but now he's full time throughout the season. He does other work in the winter. I do, too, when I can, because we need the money.'

Lauren put the knife down and turned to Grace, fingering her loose hair and winding it round her finger. 'Did you ever leave Ben when he was small . . . with anyone else, I mean, while you went out?'

Grace shook her head as she opened the fridge door and peered inside. 'How could I? There was no one, you see.'

'No one?'

'We lived in a remote part. It was very beautiful.' For a moment Grace's eyes looked dreamy. Was she remembering how it was when Ben was growing into the son she was so proud of now?

Lauren bit her lip, turning her head away so that the pain didn't show on her face. When she herself was young Dad had been there as well as Mum. They'd done things together, the three of them and Mum hadn't seemed to have a care in the world. She could see her now so clearly she could hardly bear it. It was like remembering things about a stranger.

But the boy, Stephen, hadn't any memories of his mother. And because she now knew about his existence it changed the past. She had lost it . . . for ever.

'You look pensive,' Grace said, removing the plate of chopped carrot and putting some mushrooms in its place. 'Chop those, love, and then we've finished.'

Automatically Lauren moved her knife up and down. She felt Grace glance at her once or twice, and made an effort to smile as she worked.

'You like it here, don't you, Lauren?' Grace asked when the mushrooms had been added to the huge casserole and it was ready to go into the oven.

'It's fine.'

'You're doing well, dear.' Grace straightened, and turned to her, gently smiling. 'Ben told me how good you are at helping, and joining in on the hikes. You're just what we need, someone to accompany the youngsters and get them enthusiastic about joining in. We're short-staffed, you see. Joanna's good with them, of course, but they do need people their own age.'

'Oh yes, Joanna,' Lauren said with a leaden tone in her voice.

The smile went from Grace's face. She nodded, and busied herself taking the bulging liner out of the pedal bin.

Lauren ran her hand over the work surface. She thought of the way Joanna coped with everything thrown at her, whatever it was, without grumbling. 'Joanna's so good at everything.'

Grace looked at her swiftly. 'Don't let Joanna get to you, Lauren. She doesn't mean anything.'

'Dad likes her.'

Grace was silent as she crushed an empty carton and rammed it into the bag of rubbish to carry outside to the dustbin. On her return she looked serious. 'I've been thinking,' she said. 'It's lonely here for you, Lauren, and we need extra help here in the kitchen. I was wondering . . . you haven't a friend who wants a holiday job, have you?'

Lauren's eyes lit up. 'You really mean it?'

'You have?' Grace smiled.

'Vicki!'

'Would she come?'

'I could ask her. It's brilliant.'

Grace looked round the kitchen to see if anything else needed doing and then followed Lauren out into the main room. 'Is she on the phone, Lauren? Better ask your dad if it's a good idea first, though.'

'It'd be great having her here. Really great. Thanks for suggesting it.' Lauren looked around the room. 'Do you want me to lay the tables?'

Grace laughed. 'Not for another hour at least. Go off and phone your friend. And, Lauren . . . good luck! Tell her we need her desperately.'

Lauren laughed too as she went off to find her father. It was good of Grace to suggest her having a friend here. They'd have a great time together, and it would help Grace out, too. Suddenly she realised how much she was missing Vicki, with her down-to-earth good humour and the way she had of cutting everyone down to size.

Vicki would come if she had to go down to Bristol and bring her back herself!

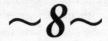

~*8*~

'You've simply got to come, Vicki.' Lauren's voice on the phone was firm, but inside she was a dithering mass of uncertainty. Bristol was so far away. Would her friend think it was worth all the expense of getting here? 'I'm desperate, I tell you.'

Behind her the office door opened. She turned slightly, motioning silence to her father. He raised his eyebrows at her, mouthing the words, 'Any good?'

'Dad's here now,' said Lauren. 'He wants you to come, too.'

Mr Wainwright gave a huge grin as he seated himself at his desk.

Vicki's voice sounded indecisive. 'But how do I get there?'

'Easy. Train to Leeds, and Dad said he'll pick you up there. Oh do say you'll come, Vicki. We need you here.'

'Any developments yet with you-know-what?'

Lauren glanced swiftly at her father. 'Well, sort of. Vicki, listen. You've got to come. Please . . .'

'I'll think about it.'

'Now. You've got to say *now*.'

'I'll have to ask Mum. You know me, Lauren. The usual cash flow problems.'

'So come and earn some here. What can I say to persuade you?' Lauren looked despairingly at her father.

'I'll talk to her,' he said.

She passed the phone across. His voice sounded soothing and totally convincing as he explained the position. Lauren clutched her hands together, willing Vicki to agree. Until Grace suggested it, she hadn't thought it was possible to have her friend here so soon. Now she couldn't live with the thought that it might not happen.

At last he put the phone down. 'Of course this has to be discussed with her mother. But Vicki sounds hopeful.'

'Oh Dad!' Lauren's face lit up in a smile. 'When will she come?'

'She'll phone back later.' He got up, and rubbed his hands together. 'We'd better find Grace and see what she's got lined up in the way of accommodation.'

Lauren was surprised. 'But won't Vicki stay at the cottage?'

'Maybe. Maybe not. See what Grace says.'

Lauren flew down the stairs ahead of him and up into the clubhouse where Grace was arranging some boating magazines in a rack. 'I've been thinking,' she said as she placed the last one in position. 'The small room next to mine will be suitable for your friend, Lauren.' She stood up straight and smiled from her to Arnold as he followed his daughter into the room.

'No problem.'

He picked up one of the magazines and stood with it in his hand. 'Let's hope Vicki's a help to you, Grace,' he said. 'You do far too much.'

She brushed aside his words with a flick of her head, but there was a softening about her mouth and her eyes looked bright. 'You haven't seen the accommodation wing yet, have you, Arnold? Come and have a look. You can help me get Vicki's room ready for her, Lauren, if you like.'

Her calm assumption that Vicki would be coming was just what Lauren needed. They collected the bedding on the way.

Grace threw open the door of the end room. Its brightly curtained windows gave a fine view of their cottage with the hillside above. Lauren put down her cargo of blankets.

'It's small,' Grace said. 'But there's a fitted wardrobe and a chest of drawers. I'll bring a chair up presently. What do you think, Lauren?'

Before she could answer there was the sound of footsteps, and Joanna appeared in the doorway. She looked surprised.

'We hope to have Lauren's friend coming to work with us,' Grace explained quietly as she moved the blankets from the bed to the top of the chest of drawers.

Joanna raised her eyebrows. 'Great. I haven't had any free time for ages.' She was looking straight at Arnold.

Turning her back on them both, Grace began to spread a sheet on the bed.

'Can you come at once, Arnold?' Joanna said rather breathlessly. 'Something's cropped up.'

As they left together Grace said nothing. With Lauren's help she worked swiftly. With the bed made the room looked comfortable and inviting.

It seemed ages before the phone call came from Vicki. 'I'm coming,' she said. This time her voice boomed down the phone and, laughing, Lauren had to hold the receiver away from her ear.

'There's so much to tell you,' she cried. 'When will you get here?'

'The train gets in at Leeds at eight tomorrow night. Is that all right? I'll walk if I have to.'

Vicki, walk? That was a laugh. 'It's getting on for thirty miles,' Lauren told her, giggling. 'I'd like to see you.'

'You will see me . . . on Leeds station tomorrow night,' Vicki said confidently. Then her voice changed. 'Be sure you get there in time, won't you, Lauren?'

They didn't see Vicki at first. After the quietness of Alderdale, the station seemed like a circus when they got there the next evening. They'd had trouble parking, and by the time her father slipped into a place vacated at the last moment Lauren was breathless with frustration. Screwing her eyes up, she looked anxiously towards the mass of bodies surging from the platform.

The noise hurt her ears. For a dizzy moment she thought Vicki hadn't come. 'There she is!' she cried at last.

Laden with a suitcase that bulged alarmingly, Vicki came stumping towards them. The straps of a huge bag were slipping from her shoulders. She paused to hump the straps up and flick her dark hair away from her face as she gazed around. Then she saw them, and her eyes lit up with relief.

Lauren ran forward. She'd never been so pleased to see anyone in her life. 'I thought we'd never find you, Vicki.'

'Phew!' Vicki dumped her suitcase and moved her bag from one shoulder to the other. She looked just the same, as rosy-cheeked and bright-eyed as ever.

Mr Wainwright picked up the case, smiling and looking as pleased to see Vicki as Lauren was herself. 'Let's get out of this madhouse, girls.'

'The journey took ages,' Vicki said as she walked beside them. 'I thought they'd moved Leeds off the map.'

Lauren giggled. It was great having Vicki here.

They could hardly stop talking as they piled into the car. 'Now tell me everything,' Vicki demanded as they set off. 'What's it like living in the wilds?'

Lauren giggled again. It was like it always used to be, having Vicki beside her on the back seat of the car. She told her about the cottage, and the room that had been got ready for her in the clubhouse next to Grace, and about the different activities she herself had to take part in.

'Not me, I hope,' Vicki said, sitting upright and then sliding down in her seat again as they swerved round a bend. 'You know me. I'll have them all falling down mountains and drowning in the lake!'

Mr Wainwright gave a deep-throated laugh. 'As long as you don't poison them, too, Vicki, we'll do all right. Grace'll put you in the picture as to your duties. In the kitchen, mostly.'

Vicki gave an elaborate sigh of relief that set them laughing again. 'So, who else is on the team beside us three and this Grace?' she asked.

'Joanna Drew.' Lauren spoke quickly before her father had time to answer. 'And Ben. Grace is his mother. And Richard is going to stay on as an extra leader when his group leave on Sunday because we're short of help. You'll meet them all when we get there.'

'What sort of people come then, Lauren? More fellas than girls, I hope. I need a bit of action.'

Mr Wainwright chuckled. 'Don't worry, Vicki. There

will be plenty of action, but not the sort you have in mind.'

Lauren laughed, too. 'It's about half and half, boys and girls. At least it is with the group from Misterdale we have in now. They come from near Newcastle, and they're great. They're a church group.'

Vicki made a face at Lauren, and then asked more questions about the activities.

It seemed as if they'd exhausted all their news by the time they reached Alderdale at last and bumped down the drive to draw up outside the clubhouse. However there was still plenty to say when the luggage had been unloaded and carried up to Vicki's room and she'd been introduced to the others.

Grace smiled at her, looking as pleased to see her as if she'd been her own friend. 'There's coffee and sandwiches,' she said. 'Help yourselves, girls, and then I expect Vicki would like to unpack and get settled.'

It was dark outside now, and they couldn't see the hillside or the cottage. Lauren pulled the curtains across Vicki's window and then sat on the bed and watched her undo her suitcase and tip everything out onto the floor in her usual chaotic fashion.

'Not hard to see why money's tight at the moment,' Vicki said in satisfaction. 'There's a new shop opened in Freer Street. Terrific gear at good prices.' She bent to pick up an olive and cerise shirt, and held it against her. 'Like it, Lauren?'

Lauren smiled. 'It's great.'

As Vicki thumped down on both knees to create some sort of order, Lauren began to tell her about the letter the York solicitor had sent.

Vicki sat back on her heels and gave a low whistle. 'Wow! Action stations. Quick work, wasn't it?'

Lauren bent down to pick up some books. She sat with them in her hand, looking down at them without seeing them. Yes, it was quick, too quick for her peace of mind. Who but Uncle Dave could have given their address away? But he didn't know this one because they hadn't been in touch with him since making the decision to move north.

Vicki held a pile of T-shirts tight against her, and looked at Lauren expectantly . . . 'What did you say? Are you going to see him?'

Lauren shook her head.

Vicki's eyes shone. 'But you must, you really must.'

'No way.'

'Why not?'

'Dad wrote back at once, refusing. I told you, Vicki, I'm not going to see him, ever.'

Vicki threw the T-shirts into the drawer, and scooped up some jeans. 'You're crazy.'

Lauren shrugged. 'It's not right, I know it isn't. Dad agrees. At least he didn't say he didn't.'

'But you've *got* to let him come. I'll make you change your mind, just see if I don't!'

It sounded as if Vicki was joking, but Lauren wasn't too sure. There was something deadly serious about the look in her friend's eyes. But no one was going to make her do something she felt was wrong, not even Vicki. 'Mum cut him right out of her life,' she said. 'So it's up to me to do the same.'

Vicki muttered something as she slung the jeans over the chair. 'So what happens now?'

'Dad says that's the end of it, and I know he's right. But Vicki, suppose the boy takes no notice and comes to look for me anyway? What would you do?'

'You mean about coming to find you after you said

no . . . or if I was you?'

'Both, really.'

'Well, you know me. Nosey as they come. I'd want to meet him right away . . . see what he's like. I keep telling you . . .'

'And if you were him?'

'The same of course. I'd be here like a shot. Couldn't keep away.'

'That's what I was afraid of at first. But you see, Richard gave me his New Testament and . . .'

But Vicki wasn't interested in Richard at the moment. She sprang up, her cheeks flushed. 'I've got it, Lauren. It's brilliant. Get your brother to come. You don't have to let on you're you. That way you can see what he's like and . . .'

Lauren looked startled. 'You mean we'd change places?'

'It'd be a laugh, wouldn't it?'

'Now it's you being crazy. Anyway it wouldn't work. We'd have to put everyone else in the picture and I couldn't bear that . . . especially Joanna.'

'Joanna? The tall one with the long face who prances about acting young?'

Lauren nodded. 'I don't like her. She's so . . . so . . . but Dad thinks she's all right.' Her eyes clouded. 'He's changed since we got here, Vicki. He never used to be so interested in women. He doesn't seem like my dad any more.'

Vicki looked wise as she went down on her knees again. 'It must be the mid-life crisis.'

'He's not *that* old.'

'Neither is Joanna . . . really. I hope I can do as much as she seems to when I'm her age. All right, you needn't laugh.'

Vicki got up from the floor, stretched and looked down at her plump figure.

'I'm not laughing.' Lauren pulled down the corners of her mouth with her fingers.

Vicki slumped down on the bed beside her and looked sympathetic.

Lauren sighed. 'Even if you were tall and slim like her, you wouldn't run after married men, would you?'

'Your dad's not married any more.'

Lauren was silent for a moment. He wasn't, but she couldn't take it in, even now. Mum was so much a part of their lives and always would be. 'Joanna won't leave him alone,' she said at last.

Vicki grinned suddenly. 'You need me here. I can see that.'

'I *told* you . . .'

A sudden loud tapping on the door made them both jump. 'Hey, you two, how about getting some sleep? It's an early start tomorrow. You'll never get up in time.' It was Joanna's husky voice.

'Sorry!' Vicki called cheerfully.

Startled, Lauren glanced at her watch. 'It's gone ten-thirty,' she whispered.

Vicki lowered her voice, too. 'What's special about tomorrow?'

Lauren shrugged as she got off the bed. 'Nothing. Group activities in the morning . . . sailing, hiking, canoeing . . .'

Vicki shuddered as she struggled to her feet and bent to scoop the rest of her belongings off the floor. 'What about this Richard then, Lauren,' she said in a loud whisper. 'What's he like?'

'Ssh!' Lauren hissed. 'Not so loud. Richard's not our age. He's one of the older leaders.'

'And Ben?'

Lauren felt warm colour flood her face, and turned away so her friend wouldn't see. 'See you tomorrow,' she whispered as she let herself out of the room.

The light was on in the cottage. Lauren flew up the track towards it. She felt such an overwhelming desire to read more from Richard's book that she refused the offer of coffee from her father who was standing by the cooker with the kettle already in his hand.

'Richard's lent me something special, Dad,' she said rather shyly. 'I'm going to read it now. It's his New Testament. And I've had this lovely feeling. I *know* everything's going to work out.'

Her father smiled, a sad expression in his eyes. 'He's a good man, Richard. Off you go then, lass. We've had a full day.' He put the kettle down again. 'I'm tired too. The best place is bed, for both of us.'

~9~

In spite of Joanna's gloomy warnings, Lauren was up no later than usual next morning, and breakfast was ready by the time her father came into the kitchen.

He yawned, rubbing his hand across his eyes as if he hadn't had a very good night. He grinned as he saw the table, though, and the years seemed to drop from him.

'You seem bright this morning, lass,' he said as he seated himself. 'What's that you've got there?'

Lauren smiled at the small book she had placed beside her plate. 'It's the New Testament Richard gave me. I've been reading it, Dad. Do you remember the verses like poetry Grandad used to like?'

The memory seemed to please him, and she quoted the verses about the flowers flowering in the desert to glorify God. 'That started me off, Dad, and Richard and I got talking. Dad, why don't you read it too?'

'Maybe I will.'

Lauren smiled, knowing he would if he said so. 'I can't wait to see Vicki,' she told him happily as she made the tea. 'It's great having her here. Grace is pleased, isn't she?'

He poured cereal into his bowl and tipped in some milk. 'She works too hard, does Grace. Vicki is just what she needs. I hope things work out.'

A tap on the window and the postman's friendly shout had Lauren leaping up to open the door. It was hard not to glance fearfully at the letters as her father took them from her.

'Aren't you going to look at them, Dad?' she asked as he placed them to one side and continued his breakfast.

He looked at her, a frown between his eyes. 'Time enough later. Stop worrying, lass. It's over and done with now. And didn't you just say that everything's going to be all right for us?'

She smiled, ashamed of having doubted it. 'It still bugs me a bit,' she confessed as she pushed the marmalade pot towards him.

'Then we'll have to do something about it. We can't have you looking as if you've seen a ghost every time the postman comes.'

'But what, Dad? What can we do?'

They had been through this sort of thing before. The first time, after Uncle Dave had told them the shocking news about the boy, they'd taken off for the north. This time there was nothing they could do except sit tight and believe that everything would work out.

Vicki was in the kitchen, washing up, when Lauren got down to the clubhouse. She looked as at home as if she had been there all the time. She had a large white apron over her jeans and jersey, and her plump face shone with good humour.

There wasn't much chance to talk though, because of the early start planned for the group going caving, and all the bustle of getting the other groups organised.

'Canoeing for you, Lauren,' Ben told her, running his hands through his dark hair. 'I know it's new to you, but you can learn with the group today.' He looked at her uncertainly. 'That is . . . if you feel like it?'

She took a deep breath, and let it out slowly. Ben was still looking anxious, and she gave a huge grin to show she could tackle anything.

Canoeing was different, but nice. When it was her turn she got into the canoe as she had been shown, and with a few sure strokes of the paddle, was out on the water. She liked the feeling of being able to control her speed so easily on the calm surface of the lake. The roll over though was a different matter. She'd never be able to handle that, she thought in dismay. But by the time Ben announced the break for lunch she had even managed to get herself to roll right over in the water and to come up safely on the other side.

'Great,' he told her, smiling, as she came up, dripping lake water from her face and hair. 'You can have some more practice this afternoon while they're doing the orienteering if you like.'

She grinned back, suddenly confident and wanting more.

They arrived late for lunch. Ben waited for her while she rushed up to the cottage to change into dry clothes, and together they climbed the clubhouse steps and found a spare space at one of the tables where Vicki joined them.

'Phew!' she said, leaning both arms on the table. 'Talk about feeding the five thousand. It's enough to put you off eating for the rest of your life.'

Ben smiled as she reached for another roll to eat with her soup. He hadn't said much to Vicki yet, or she to him. Once or twice Lauren caught her friend looking at him, sizing him up. She'd hear soon enough what Vicki thought about him.

Ben soon finished his lunch and was off, clipboard in hand, to check about some new arrivals expected later in the day.

Vicki helped herself to a bag of crisps. She broke open the packet and began to eat as if she hadn't had food for a week. 'You got more people coming?' she asked in surprise, crunching away. 'The place is overrun with bodies already.'

Lauren frowned. 'Dad didn't say anything. Perhaps they've just booked in.'

'Can they do that?' Vicki screwed up the crisp bag, and looked at Lauren wide-eyed. 'You don't think . . . ?'

The same thought had occurred to Lauren. She got up and scraped her chair back. 'Won't be a minute, Vicki. See you!'

Ben had come down from the office with his clip-board, so she knew Dad was still up there. He was working at his desk as she went in. She felt a little foolish as she sat down on the chair opposite him. Ben hadn't said one person was coming on his own. She was over-reacting again!

Her father looked up, smiling. 'So the canoeing went well?' He scratched his head with the end of his pen. 'Some more of the same this afternoon? Joanna tells me she can cope with the orienteering now she doesn't have to help Grace as well. It looks as if Vicki's a success in the kitchen. It was a waste having Joanna tied up indoors.'

Lauren nodded. 'She did caving this morning.'

Her father smiled. 'Joanna's a great one for coping

with everything anyone throws at her.'

'Dad . . . isn't the place full? I mean . . . Ben said some more people were coming.'

He rustled some papers until he found the one he wanted. 'Four girls from Southport. We can fit them in all right. No problem. You weren't thinking . . . ?'

She bit her lip. Of course she was. Why was it so hard not to let these doubts come sweeping over her when she knew she should have more trust?

Her father laid the papers in a neat pile to one side, looking grave. 'I've been doing some thinking myself, lass. It's a possibility there could be a follow-up to this business even though I made your decision plain in my letter. Anyway you're a bag of nerves about it, whether it'll happen or not. I made up my mind that someone else should know what's afoot in case we're not around.'

She looked at him in horror. 'Oh no, Dad, you're not going to . . .'

'Someone who can cope. Someone who'll know what to do should anything arise. It's for your sake, Lauren.'

He'd done it already. She could tell by the way he was looking at her! She felt icy cold. 'Dad, you can't. It's our secret . . .'

He looked at her steadily. 'We don't want any more secrets . . . do we, lass? Think on it.'

She stared at him, white-faced. Secrets . . . deep dark secrets that tore your family apart. She wanted none of them either, but this was different. 'You should have asked first. It's wrong, telling her behind my back. And now she'll . . .' Her voice trembled.

'Grace is the soul of discretion. It's safe with her.'

'Grace?' For a moment the name didn't register.

'I thought she should know. We can trust Grace.'

'But I thought . . .' Lauren felt as if the blood was

flowing back into her body where there'd been none before. She had thought it was Joanna . . . of course she had . . . and Joanna would probe and fuss and make life a misery. Grace . . . but even Grace knowing was a bad idea.

'How can I forget if everyone here knows?' she burst out.

Her father looked at her, a patient expression on his face. 'Not everybody. Only Grace, and Vicki. You don't mind Vicki knowing, do you?'

She pushed back her chair. 'Vicki's different. You shouldn't have told anyone . . .' She broke off, and then turned and ran.

She couldn't face anyone now, not even Vicki. There was this new thing to take in . . . Grace knowing. And Dad's disloyalty in telling her.

She ran blindly up the track. The cottage door stood open as she had left it when she had come up to change such a short time before. She'd had no idea then that Dad had done things behind her back . . . and now it was all being taken out of her hands. Suppose Dad hadn't thought to swear Grace to secrecy? Suppose Grace told Ben? Up to now it had all been *her* decision, *her* problem . . . but not any more.

Her wet clothes were still in the kitchen where she had dumped them. Grabbing them up, she rushed outside and began to peg them on the line. They'd all be thinking about it . . . waiting for something to happen, someone to come looking for her. She'd never be able to forget about it and go on as if nothing had happened . . .

She was so intent on what she was doing that she didn't hear Grace call out a greeting, and she gave a startled gasp as a shadow fell across the grass. She spun around.

Grace smiled pleasantly. 'Sorry to creep up on you, dear. Your dad was worried. He asked me to speak to you.'

Lauren stared at her in silence. She wanted no interference, not even from Grace.

'I'm sorry about it. I didn't ask for his confidence,' Grace said quietly.

'He had no right to tell you!'

Grace gave a little shrug. 'He had his reasons, and I think they're good ones.'

'So why did he tell me I'd no need to worry?' Lauren picked up the peg bag and held it to her like a shield. Her eyes were stormy. 'And now he tells you, and you'll tell Ben and . . .'

'Tell Ben? Of course not. Your father knows that I'm always around the Centre, that I'd be aware of anyone coming in. Can't you see, Lauren, that I'm the obvious person? I'd know immediately what's going on, when the others wouldn't.'

It sounded reasonable, but Lauren wasn't convinced. She took a deep breath and moved towards the cottage door. Inside, she stood for a moment leaning against the wall in the passage until she heard Grace come to the door too.

'Please, Lauren, don't let this upset you.' With the light behind her, Grace's fair hair stood out like a halo. 'I wanted you to know that this wasn't any doing of mine, that's all. I have to get back now . . . but, Lauren, I'd like to say something else, if you'll let me?'

Lauren went ahead of her into the kitchen and then faced her in silence as Grace stood rather diffidently on the threshold. 'Just this . . . and then I'll go. I think you should tell Ben about it too. It'll be better coming from you. He's good at coping with anything and will keep a look out among the young people.'

'Coping!' Lauren cried. 'Everybody's good at coping. I can cope, too, if I'm given the chance.'

She pushed past Grace, hurling herself down the track to the lakeside. She would show them. She had promised to do some more canoe work with Ben this afternoon and that was exactly what she was going to do. But she wouldn't tell Ben anything.

She sat down on a spare dinghy trolley to wait for him, staring at the lake with eyes that saw nothing but that letter that had caused such havoc in her life.

It wasn't until Lauren saw movement among the tents that she got up at last. She stretched, feeling stiff and cold. A faint muddy smell was borne on the breeze. Ben still hadn't come. She began to walk up to the tents, and found that the first group of orienteerers was back. They crowded round Richard, hiding him completely, all talking at once. Extricating himself, he came towards her, smiling cheerfully.

'Care to help me check out this lot?' he called. He ran his hand through his hair, looking as hot as if he had been rushing across the hillside himself. 'With Tom not showing up yet I could use some help. He was supposed to be back by now.' He wrinkled his forehead, looking worried. Then he smiled at her. 'Ben's been looking for you, love. He'll be here in a minute.'

By the time Ben arrived ten minutes later she and Richard had checked the answers to the clues and were looking for the next group to come pouring in. Lauren glanced at Ben, feeling suddenly in the wrong, though how could that be when she had turned up and he hadn't?

'I waited ages,' she said rather defiantly, and was pleased to see an apologetic look in his eyes.

'I need to talk to you,' Ben said.

Lauren looked down at the list in her hand. 'Can't you see I'm helping Richard? The next lot'll be back soon.'

They came running in as she spoke and crowded round to have their clues checked.

Ben stood to one side, frowning. He held himself stiffly, and looked every now and again up at the clubhouse. It wouldn't hurt him to have a turn at waiting, Lauren thought as she handed back the last sheet. What did he think she had been doing down at the lakeside all that long time . . . feeding the ducks?

Richard stuck his pen in the top pocket of his white shirt. At his movement two of the buttons strained and looked as if they would pop off. 'All done now, Lauren. Clear off now if you want. Thanks for your help.'

Ben's light T-shirt had a patch of blue paint on one sleeve. He looked solemn as she came towards him as if he thought she was going to attack him.

'So . . . where were you?' she demanded.

'Why didn't you do something about it yourself, then? Just waiting for me down there like a zombie!'

His own verbal attack surprised her. She hadn't heard him react like this before. 'But I thought . . .'

'You think too much, that's your trouble. Mine, too, if it comes to that.' He turned and moved smartly towards the track that led down to the lake.

'Where are we going?' She had to run to keep up with him.

'Where d'you think? Canoeing's what you want to do, isn't it?'

'Not now. It's too late. Anyway, Richard wanted me to help him now Tom hasn't come back. Joanna went with the slowest lot so she couldn't do the checking.' She was still almost running at his side as they went down the track to the boatyard.

Near the canoe park he came to a full stop. He spun round to face her, his face dark. 'What have you been doing to my mum? She's in a right state after what you said. What's going on?'

'Nothing's going on,' Lauren cried breathlessly.

He glared at her. 'We're all in this together, running this place, whether you like it or not. We can't have undercurrents . . . people getting upset. We pull together. Understand?'

'It's not my fault!'

'So . . . whose fault is it then, hers?'

'Yes . . . no. I mean . . . Keep out of it, Ben. It's nothing to do with you!'

His eyes flashed. 'This place is everything to do with me.'

She glared at him. 'You haven't said why you didn't show up earlier.'

'Your dad wanted me. I had to go at once.'

Dad wouldn't, she thought desperately. Dad didn't . . . ?

The colour in Ben's cheeks was high, and his eyes glittered. 'Are you coming canoeing, or not?'

Angrily, she turned her back on him, and heard the swish of a canoe being pulled across the grass. Surely Dad wouldn't tell Ben as well as Grace? But no, he'd promised. She had to trust him . . . just Grace and Vicki. That's what he'd said.

~10~

Lauren shrugged her shoulders, and went up to the club-house without looking back at the lake. Let Ben get on with it if he wanted to be like that. Why should she care?

She could tell that the preparations for the evening meal were well under way by the onion and tomato smells floating towards her.

Vicki was sitting reading at a table with her feet up on a chair, looking as if she hadn't stirred since lunchtime.

'So where were you?' she demanded, glaring at Lauren over the top of her magazine. 'A fine one you are. See you, she says. Won't be long, she says. A mystery going and keeping it all to yourself. So what did your Dad say?'

'Dad?'

'You were off to find out about likely strangers, remember?'

Lauren looked at her rather bleakly. Things had changed since then, and she'd forgotten. 'Oh yes, Dad. Some girls from Southport are coming . . .'

Vicki looked disappointed. 'So . . . why not come back and tell me?'

'Something cropped up.'

Vicki looked at her hopefully as she shut the magazine sharply and dumped it on the table. Before she could say anything, though, Lauren jumped in quickly with her reason for not returning to report at once. 'Dad's told Grace. It was all supposed to be a secret, but he told Grace.'

Vicki's eyes shone, and a smile quirked the corners of her mouth. 'You don't mean it . . . that he confided in Grace and not Joanna?' She let out a low whistle. 'She won't like it, that one. There'll be repercussions.'

'You've missed the point, Vicki. Joanna won't know, but Grace knows. It's not a secret any more.'

'You mean she'll tell Ben?'

Lauren shook her head. She thought of Grace standing in the doorway, looking upset. It wasn't Grace's fault having a confidence forced on her she didn't want, but she'd quarrelled with her because of it. And with Ben too, and that hurt.

She went to the window that gave a view of the lake and stood looking out at the lone canoe moving swiftly across the surface of the water. Soon it would disappear behind the heathery arm of land that hid the distant part of the lake. Ben was moving fast, as if he wanted to get as far away as possible.

Vicki yawned, and stretched. 'Thick as thieves, aren't they, Ben and his mum?'

Lauren frowned. 'Grace promised not to tell him.'

'A mother's boy, that's Ben.'

'He's not!' A quick flush of colour stained Lauren's cheeks. Ben was never that. She thought of Ben standing in the sunshine with his dark head thrown back, organising the groups each day; of his confidence in handling the sailing dinghy and the way he taught everyone to use the canoes. He had supported his mother in the decision she made about taking up their jobs here, and did extra work in the winter to help out. Grace was lucky to have a supportive son like that.

She perched on the window ledge, swinging one leg, trying hard to hide her annoyance with Vicki.

Her friend gave a long contemplative sigh. 'He's tied to her apron strings, don't tell me he isn't.'

Lauren took a deep breath, opening her mouth to deny it hotly, and then shut it again. Vicki was like a stone wall once her mind was made up. It wouldn't do any good.

She took a quick look at the lake. No movement disturbed the calm water now. You'd never think that only a moment ago a canoe had gone flashing across with its thin wake streaming out behind.

The dull ache she felt wouldn't go away.

Vicki flicked at her magazine with one finger, watching it skim to the edge of the table. 'Ah well, you can't win 'em all!'

Lauren was silent. In spite of everything her friend came out with, she was glad to have Vicki here to bounce ideas and opinions off. Thoughts were like rubber balls. Some you caught and some you didn't. Any minute now Vicki would start up about that letter and her decision not to meet her brother. But this time she'd be ready for her.

'So, Lauren . . .' Vicki looked at her hesitantly and then seemed to make up her mind. 'What about that letter then?' Lauren leapt off the window ledge. 'No way.'

'You're crazy not to want to meet him. D'you know

that?'

'If I agreed to see him and he came here it wouldn't be fair to Dad. I won't do that to him.'

'See him on your own then. What's the solicitor's address? I'll come with you.' Vicki's face shone with eagerness.

'No way.' Mum had turned her back on her little boy. How could she go out of her way to contact him now that she was dead?

'But why not . . . ?'

'Lots of reasons.' She smiled at Vicki's stone-wall expression. 'I'll write them down for you if you like. Stick them up on your bedroom wall.'

Vicki sniggered. 'And have Joanna see them when she's prowling round?'

Lauren drew in a quick breath. Out of the corner of her eye she saw Joanna at the door. Had she heard? But there was no stopping Vicki.

At Lauren's silence Vicki turned her head too. Her face brightened. 'Coming to join us?' she asked Joanna with exaggerated friendliness.

Lauren's flush was echoed in the red that crept over the older woman's face. For once Joanna was at a loss for words. She looked from one to the other of the girls, and then withdrew swiftly.

'Vicki!' Lauren hissed. 'Shut up, will you?'

Vicki looked smug. 'I said you need me here to sort things out.'

'*That's* a matter of opinion! If you go round insulting people you won't be here much longer yourself.'

Unrepentant, Vicki grinned, but Lauren didn't smile back. It was a new feeling . . . being sorry for Joanna!

Later she wandered down to the boatyard again, unable to keep away. There was an empty space among the canoes, and she looked at it thoughtfully, winding a strand of hair round her finger.

The ache she'd felt earlier was still there.

She placed her hand on the prow of the canoe next to the space, and felt it move slightly. A canoe was light . . . no weight at all, and she knew how to use one.

Without another thought she started to pull it down to the water's edge. In a matter of moments it was afloat and she was clambering in. She extricated the paddle and was away.

Concentrating hard, she used the paddle gently at first, gaining confidence with every stroke. She didn't have time even to wonder if anyone saw her take to the water, before she was well away from shore and making for the point of land that jutted out into the water.

Once round it, the end of the lake seemed very far away. The heathery hills at the end seemed like the remote slopes of a mountain range and the curlew calling in the distance sent a cold shiver down her spine. For the first time she wondered what Ben's reaction would be when he saw her following him.

Raising her paddle out of the water she let herself drift as she scanned the surface for the other canoe. He had to be somewhere out there. She'd seen him set off down the lake, so where was he?

Her relief when she saw him was enormous.

As he came skimming towards her she saw the anger on his face, and realised for the first time that she wasn't wearing a buoyancy aid.

'Don't you know the rules?' he called. 'Go back at once!'

She tried to turn quickly, but the canoe wobbled alarmingly. The next second she was floundering and gasping in the water with Ben's urgent voice shouting something she couldn't hear. Then he, too, was beside her. He grabbed her, and his own buoyancy aid kept them afloat, but only just.

'I can swim,' she spluttered.

Both canoes seemed to have moved further away.

Quickly he unzipped his buoyancy aid. 'Get your arms into this, and then get back to the canoe.'

It wasn't easy, but she managed, and then did as he said. She seemed too high in the water to move as swiftly as Ben was doing, unencumbered.

By the time she got there he was in his canoe and paddling it towards hers. Leaning over, he tried to hold it still for her to struggle into it. Desperately she tried, again and again.

'It's no good,' she gasped frantically. 'I can't. It's impossible. There's no way for me to get a grip.'

Ben could see that for himself. He glanced towards the shore. 'Swim for it, then. I'll get your canoe back to the landing stage. Get round there as fast as you can.'

She set off, feeling like a whale in the bulky buoyancy aid. She was glad that the clubhouse was out of sight behind the headland. No one would have seen what had happened even if they'd been looking.

Her teeth were chattering by the time she reached shallow water, and her legs felt like jelly as she waded ashore. Ben had reached the tip of the headland now, paddling slowly with one hand and holding the prow of her canoe alongside his with the other.

She set off running and slithering round the shore of the lake, her feet squelching in her wet trainers. By the time she arrived at the landing stage he was nearing it too, and she rushed into the water to help bring the canoes to dry land.

But Ben had other ideas. 'Get in,' he said.

'I . . . I can't.' She seemed to have lost her nerve, but she knew she had to do it. Somehow she managed, but she didn't know how.

She moved slowly out onto the lake, concentrating hard.

'Now turn and come back,' Ben shouted.

This time she managed without mishap. She swung her legs out as she reached him, and he helped her out. Unzipping her buoyancy aid, she pulled it off and put it on the canoe.

As soon as the canoes were on shore she turned a miserable face to him.

Seeing it, his expression softened just a little, but she couldn't blame him for being mad. First she quarrelled with his mother and then went out on the lake on her own and landed up in trouble.

He took a step towards her, caught hold of her arms and held them tightly. 'Why did you come after me like that?' he demanded.

'I was afraid. I wanted you to be all right.'

His face was close to hers, and she gave a little sob. 'You were out of sight, round the headland, and I was concerned about you, Ben.'

'Lauren!' She felt the soft brush of his lips on her cheek before he released her.

'Don't you ever feel like going off on your own sometimes?' he asked, his face turned away.

'Sometimes.'

'That's what I was doing. But I'm experienced on the water, and you're not. You should have had more sense.'

'It's your fault,' she burst out. 'Not being here this afternoon. Richard's worried about Tom. He was supposed to be back by now. And I am too . . .' She broke off, biting her lip.

'Tom?' Ben looked at her darkly as he lifted his canoe. 'What's he got to do with it?'

She shrugged. 'Nothing really, but everything's going wrong, Ben. I . . . I'm sorry I quarrelled with your mum. And . . . thanks for rescuing me.'

He carried the canoe to its position and came back for hers. He didn't look at her, but she could see he was upset now. She was upset, too, at having quarrelled with Grace. Couldn't he see that?

He muttered something to himself which she couldn't catch.

'It's not . . .' she began, but then stopped, miserably. She couldn't make anyone understand anything. It was best not to try.

She stood looking at him for a moment more as he checked the canoes were safe, and then turned and walked slowly up the track.

He didn't follow her.

Lauren didn't feel like joining in with the crowd in the clubhouse later in the evening. Vicki seemed quite at home, though, helping to select tapes to play, and didn't notice her slip out. Silence was what she needed to enable her to get a few things in perspective.

She wandered down to the lake, found a fallen log on the other side of the group of ash trees for a seat, and got the New Testament out of her pocket.

For a moment she sat with it in her hands, finding solace in the calmness of the water in front of her and the soft evening light on the hills. Her quarrel with Ben, if that was what it was, had shaken her more than she knew. She thought of the brush of his lips on her cheek. It must have meant something to him, having her there just at that moment. She wished he was here now so they could talk about things, but no one came down the track to join her and the deep silence was real.

Then she began to read. She always turned to Matthew's gospel now because that's where it had fallen open that first time. It talked of entering by the narrow gate, 'But the gate to life is narrow and the way that leads to it is hard.' She bit her lip thoughtfully as she looked up at the expanse of hillside on the other side of the lake. Nothing narrow about that, or the wide expanse of water in front of her. In the exhilaration of sailing and skimming across the surface in her canoe she had felt an uplift of something wonderful that seemed to be an answer to her prayer. She longed to experience it again, but something felt wrong now.

She looked down again at the words in front of her, and read some more. 'Do for others what you want them to do for you: this is the meaning of the Law of Moses and of the teachings of the prophets.' Well, that was only common sense, wasn't it? She couldn't disagree with that whether she believed in God or not. And she wasn't at all sure yet that she did.

So what about Grace? She must make things right with her as soon as she could . . . now, even. Perhaps then she would feel happier about everything, and lose this small, dull ache that troubled her.

She got up, and stretched, and then went back to the clubhouse, looking for Grace. To her disappointment she had already retired to bed.

'She works hard, does Grace,' her father told her. 'Are you all right, Lauren?'

She nodded as she let him draw her out onto the balcony away from the noise inside. When they found a quiet corner she held the New Testament out to him wordlessly.

He took it, rubbing his fingers over the cover. 'From the look of its battered cover someone's been reading this a lot,' he said, opening it. 'For Richard on his ninth birthday from his loving mother,' he read.

Lauren snatched it back, and looked at it, appalled. 'But he gave it to me!'

Mr Wainwright smiled. 'Richard's one of the best.'

'But his mother gave it to him when he was a little boy. How could he think of giving it away?'

'He must have wanted you to have it, lass.'

'He said that if he gave it to me he would have it, too . . .' She broke off, beginning now to get an inkling of what he meant. Maybe if she read it, and believed it, then it would mean as much to him as if he still had it. She felt humble, suddenly.

'I want to talk to you about it, Dad,' she said.

But before she could say any more Joanna came leaping out through the door, saw the two of them and paused. 'So there you are, Arnold. Mind if I join you? Something needs sorting out in tomorrow's programme.'

She drew up another chair. Lauren closed the New Testament hurriedly as her father gave her a wry grin. It seemed as if the interruption was deliberate, but she wasn't sure. Joanna had a job to do like the rest of them, and appeared to be showing a sense of responsibility. Lauren gazed at her as Joanna told her father what was wrong, and then scraped her chair back and stood up.

'There's coffee brewing inside, Arnold,' she said, 'Coming?'

He could hardly refuse. All the same Lauren followed them inside with a sense of having been pushed into the background, which she tried hard to ignore.

~11~

Lauren couldn't help feeling a flicker of compassion for Joanna next day when she and Vicki were helping sort out the caving equipment on the grass in front of the clubhouse. Vicki picked up a helmet and stuck it on top of her dark head.

'There's no time to mess about,' Joanna said. 'Get a move on, Vicki. We need the helmets over here to go in the van when it comes. Or are you planning to take over instead of me today?'

Vicki flashed her a triumphant smile as she twirled round, still with the helmet on her head. 'Good idea. What d'you think, everyone?'

The cheer that went up was deafening. Lauren, glancing at Joanna, saw a dull flush creep over her face.

Vicki grinned. Then she took the helmet off and threw it on the pile. 'Oh well, folks, I'd be no use anyway. Food's the only thing I know much about.'

'You can say that again,' someone joked, and the tension relaxed as good-natured quips flew about.

As everyone got themselves sorted out Lauren saw her father come down the steps, a list in his hand.

He frowned as he came up to her. 'What was all that about, lass?'

'It's all right, Dad, really.' Lauren picked up a map and started to fold it. 'It's just . . . well, Vicki doesn't like Joanna much. It's sorted out now.'

He didn't say anything, but his glance seemed to rest on Joanna. She looked across at him, and smiled.

'Listen, everyone,' he announced. 'There's been a hitch. Ben's phoned from Rawthwaite. He'll be late with the van. Everyone meet here in half an hour. OK?'

Lauren tucked the map into her rucksack and followed Vicki up the clubroom steps, hesitating at the top as she saw Grace come out onto the balcony.

Grace saw her, and smiled. She had a cloth in her hand and began to wipe the top of the balustrade. Lauren bit her lip. Now was her chance. She didn't like feeling at odds with Grace, and Grace didn't deserve any unpleasantness because of something she couldn't help.

She cleared her throat. 'Yesterday . . . I didn't mean it . . .' she began. 'I mean . . . it was a shock, you see, knowing Dad had told you . . .'

Grace came forward at once, and the shadow in her eyes vanished. 'You heard Ben's going to be late back? It'll give us time for a coffee. Just the two of us, love.'

She moved quickly to the kitchen, and then came back with two mugs on a tray.

'The kettle was boiling,' she said in explanation as she set the tray down on the floor and perched on the balcony edge with a mug in her hand. 'Vicki's there seeing to things and we've time to spare.'

Lauren sat down too. 'Afterwards I thought . . .'

'It's done, my dear. I'll put it right out of my

mind . . .'

'It's all right, really. Dad's only told you, no one else.'

The slight pink tinge that flushed Grace's checks made her look quite young. Her eyes shone. For the first time Lauren realised that Grace wasn't only Ben's mother but a person, too, with her own hopes and problems. She picked up her mug of coffee and took a sip. As the warmth slid down her throat she felt an answering warmth deep inside her. She had a friend in Grace, just as she had in Vicki . . . but different, oh so different! Did that mean she was two different people herself?

'You said that your coming here was an answer to prayer,' Lauren said rather diffidently. 'Did you really mean it?'

Grace smiled. 'I had this very strong feeling that it was the right thing to do. Yes, I meant it. I hope that it was the right thing for you and your father to come here to us, love. I know how it feels to lose someone you love.'

'Ben's father? Did it take you a long time to get used to being on your own with Ben?'

Grace shrugged. 'There was a lot to keep me busy, fortunately. Having a lot to think about helps too.'

Lauren stared thoughtfully at the mug in her hand. 'It's hard to get used to, isn't it, someone dying?' She thought of her father, who had been immersed in work since they'd got here. She had something else to get used to, too, the fact that Mum hadn't told her about her first marriage. That was the painful thing, coming to terms with that.

'I'm glad Dad chose to tell you,' she said.

Grace smiled again, sitting quite still with both hands round her coffee mug. She gazed dreamily out over the lake.

Lauren sipped her coffee, half expecting to hear the

sound of the van coming down the track. But there was only the murmur of distant voices and lark song high above them. She saw, now, that her over-reaction yesterday had been stupid.

'It was so obvious for Dad to tell you,' she said. 'Everyone else is out most of the time. Only you're here . . .'

Grace gave a slight jerk, and a drop of coffee spilled. She got out her hanky and dabbed it briskly. 'They're only old jeans,' she said. 'Not to worry.' Draining the rest of her coffee she put the mug down on the tray and stood up. 'You're with Ben and the canoeing group today, Lauren, aren't you?'

Lauren nodded. She didn't know whose idea it was that she should go with his group, or whether it was a good idea after his reaction to her yesterday.

'I know he's anxious you should go caving,' Grace said. 'But things didn't work out that way today because he wants to take you himself . . . with someone well-qualified too, of course.'

Obviously he hadn't told his mother that the two of them had fallen out. Vicki was wrong about Ben and Grace being as thick as thieves. She had known that anyway, but here was extra proof.

When Ben returned they set about organising the canoeing down at the lake. Ben didn't look at her as he divided the group into two: one for himself, of the more advanced canoeists, and the other for Lauren to accompany, together with one of the Misterdale leaders.

The sky was overcast today, and a stinging wind ruffled her hair as she stepped into the canoe allocated to her.

In spite of feeling at odds with Ben, the morning went

well. Lauren enjoyed skimming over the water again, just as she had at first yesterday. It was great knowing she was beginning to be of use in the activities. She didn't even mind another practice roll over, because it was all part of the job.

And yet she still had a dull ache deep down, even though she had made things right with Grace. Something was still wrong, and she didn't know what it was.

At lunchtime she and Ben sat at the same table, a little apart from the others. The awkwardness between them seemed to have vanished in the necessity of getting on with the job. Seeing them, Vicki grimaced at Lauren, shrugged her shoulders and joined the group arguing about caving at the next table.

Ben bit deep into his cheese roll. 'Like another sailing lesson later on?' he asked as he finished his mouthful.

Lauren's eyes shone. 'I'll need to get another change of clothes organised first. Ben . . . I'm sorry about things yesterday. Your mum's great. It's all right between us now, and you've no need to worry.'

He smiled, a slight flush tingeing his cheek. She felt an answering glow in her own face, as if she had said more than she meant. But how could that be when she had only told him about making things up with Grace?

After lunch they did some more canoeing with another group, and then Ben looked round for Lauren.

'Still game to sail?' he asked, as he saw her waiting by the gate into the boatyard.

She nodded. Vicki had wanted her to help prepare the evening meal when the canoeing finished, but Grace had come to her rescue and insisted that she have another sailing lesson so that soon she would be capable of teaching others and of being more use at Alderdale.

This time Ben let her take over the helm for a while.

The feeling of power it gave her as the sailing dinghy responded to her slightest movement awed Lauren into total silence. It was so easy to make a slight mistake, and she knew what that could mean. She had no wish to end up in the lake again, even though Ben had promised her a capsize practice at a later date.

They moved swiftly down the length of the lake, Lauren's knuckles white as she held the tiller. She was aware of Ben, beside her, doing all that was necessary for the crew to do, and then it was time to go about and tack all the way back up the lake again.

He took over the helm as they neared the boatyard shore, giving her a grunt of approval as they carefully changed places.

It was an anti-climax coming in so slowly and carefully after the exhilaration of the sailing.

As she removed her life-jacket, Lauren glanced at Ben, wanting to tell him something of what it meant to her, but not quite knowing how to start.

'Have you been reading that book?' he asked, as they settled the boat on the trolley and started to pull it up to the yard.

'Book?' Lauren almost stumbled in her surprise.

'You need to understand the theory of sailing too, to make a good sailor.'

'Oh, the book on sailing.' She remembered about it now, but couldn't think where she had put the book he had lent her. 'I'll look at it after tea,' she promised.

'There won't be time then. Remember the mini-treasure hunt Joanna's setting up? And after that's the Open Air Service.'

She had forgotten that for a moment. Dad had told her something about it at breakfast, that it was to be held down on the shore of the lake if the weather was good and on the balcony of the clubhouse if wet.

She wondered how many would turn up, and was surprised to find a crowd of them going down the track when the treasure hunt had finished.

The wind had died down, and most of the clouds cleared. In fact it was a lovely evening, very still and with a hint of rose-pink in the sky over the hills in the west. Ben had been busy working on the boats while Joanna's treasure hunt was in progress, and now he came across to where everyone was settling down on the grass and waiting for Richard. Lauren and Vicki sat side by side on Vicki's anorak, and Ben came to join them.

Lauren's eyes were fixed on the calm water in front of her as the service began, and Richard started to talk to them about hearing God's voice speaking through nature. The sound of the songs carried across the lake, and as the voices died away Lauren thought she could hear faint echoes among the quiet hillsides that would continue for ever. It was a lovely thought, the words they sang about the glory of God's kingdom never fading away but hiding themselves in the gathering dusk that was beginning to creep over the rising ground.

Afterwards she let the others go on ahead, loath to lose the emotion of the last quarter of an hour that had seemed to speak to her in a special, meaningful way. She turned away from the track and pushed her way up through the heather to the brow of the hill behind the boatyard, savouring the quiet evening that seemed to hold such mystery and promise. She felt close to tears with the beauty of it.

She wanted the loving memories of her mother to go on for ever in the same way that the singing seemed to echo among the hills. Why should those memories be changed by what had happened since?

~*12*~

'We never have time to talk,' Vicki grumbled.

Lauren, entering the clubhouse, hadn't seen her at first in the dazzling light. She still felt dazed, and very tired.

'Have some coffee,' Vicki said, thrusting a dripping mug at her. 'In this row you can't hear yourself think.'

Lauren took it, grateful for its warmth. All of a sudden she wanted to talk seriously to Vicki.

'Come up to the cottage,' she said. 'We can talk there.'

The ashes were still in the grate from last night. Lauren gave them a good rake round with the poker, stuck a firelighter into them with a little spurt of dust, and then piled on some of the smaller logs Dad had left ready. As she lit the match and applied it she felt the warmth and light like a blanket enfolding her. Strangely, she was no longer tired.

She sat back on her heels, and smiled at Vicki. 'Dad won't be back till later. There's so much to tell you.' But now there was time she didn't know how to start.

Vicki gave an elaborate yawn. 'Only two more days.'

Lauren was surprised. 'Two more days for what?'

'They go back to Newcastle on Sunday, don't they, the Misterdale lot? I'm going to miss them like anything.'

'Me too,' Lauren said. 'They've been great.'

Vicki leaned back in her chair. 'Get used to one lot, and off they go. It's not fair.'

'That's the way it is.' Lauren gave a little sigh, remembering Tom, who had only come for the day.

Vicki's eyes brightened. 'Who's coming next week, then? Tell me the time of their arrival, and I'll make sure to be there to view the talent. More guys than girls this time, I hope. I might stand a chance then.'

Lauren smiled. 'I wouldn't miss being here for anything, would you, Vicki?'

Her friend gave a deep shudder, and then grinned. 'All that preparing meals, all that washing up . . . Oh well, it has its compensations. Did you see the way Joanna looked at me this morning? If looks could kill!' She gave a little giggle. 'I've a lot more planned for that one.'

'She's not been so bad lately,' Lauren said, gazing thoughtfully into the fire.

'That's because you've got used to her.'

Lauren sat upright. 'Well, she and Dad aren't together as much now.'

Vicki looked wise. 'It's a blind. She's just biding her time. She'll wish she'd never set eyes on your dad by the time I've finished . . .'

'Leave her alone, Vicki. It won't do any good.'

Her friend snorted. 'You've changed. What's got into you? You'll be agreeing to meet your long-lost brother next.'

Lauren sank back with a sigh. 'How many times have I told you . . .' She broke off at Vicki's knowing look, thinking of how she had felt such a short time ago on the darkening hillside. She wished she could tell Vicki about it, and make her understand.

It had seemed an answer to her prayer, losing herself in the companionship of the group after a hard day's activities with them, during which she had experienced a freedom from fear she hadn't known for a long time. She had felt closer to her mother's memory, too, for the first time since Uncle Dave's devastating revelations.

But at Vicki's mention of her half-brother some of her newly-found freedom began to slip away, and she hastened to banish the thoughts of him from her mind. Quickly she began to talk of what Vicki had been doing, and of the barbecue arranged for Saturday night down by the lake. At once Vicki's face lit up, and they talked of nothing else until Lauren's father came in and it was time for her friend to go.

The hike planned for next day was longer than Lauren had done the first time she had accompanied Richard as leader of the hiking group. She had been disappointed not to be involved in the sailing with Ben, but was relieved not to be helping Joanna with sorting out the large storeroom beneath the clubhouse.

It felt easy and comfortable to be with Richard. His short, round figure, clad in shorts and straining T-shirt, seemed to give her confidence.

They set off round the other side of the lake where she hadn't been before. As they started to trudge uphill she was reminded vividly of that first hike and how Tom had played about with his map-reading. She still missed his cheerful good humour, and the way he had of putting everyone at their ease. Richard seemed to, as well, because he started talking about Tom as soon as they'd gone over the brow of the hill and the lake was no longer visible.

'I'll have to phone Tom and find out what's he's doing,' he said as he turned to check the rest of the group were following hard behind. 'I can't think what's got into him. Unless . . .'

'You mean something might have happened . . . like an emergency?'

Richard looked worried. He got out his handkerchief and wiped it across his moist forehead. 'His grandparents are getting on. He's very fond of them and if anything happened . . .'

Lauren was silent. Of course Tom was fond of them. All that pretence and joking hadn't disguised his real feelings.

Richard stuffed his handkerchief in the pocket of his shorts, and grinned suddenly. 'Let's not dwell on the black side, love. It's a great day. Too good for negative thoughts.'

A faint mist hung over the tops of the hills, and Lauren felt the loveliness like an ache. She thought of the psalm Richard had read to them at the service down by the lake yesterday evening: 'I look to the mountains; where will my help come from? My help will come from the Lord, who made heaven and earth.' She had asked God to help her find peace and freedom from worry, so why was there this little feeling of unease still with her that she couldn't banish, however hard she tried to concentrate on the bees working in the heather and the lark spiralling overhead with its uplifting song?

Already Richard's round face seemed to be catching the sun. 'We're going to need Tom back soon,' he said after a while. 'Did Ben tell you about taking you caving tomorrow?'

He was the second person to say this. She looked

apprehensively at him. 'Caving?'

Richard laughed at her, his eyes crinkling deep into the folds of flesh that surrounded them. 'Don't sound so worried. You'll like it.'

Lauren wasn't so sure. She thought of canoeing and sailing which she'd loved. But they were in the open air with the wind on her face. It would be different in the darkness underground. 'How do I know I'd be any good?' she asked.

'You don't, love, till you've tried it. It's good for you to do something you're afraid of, though.' He grinned suddenly. 'You won't be taken anywhere you can't cope with.'

Lauren looked unconvinced. 'How many of us'll be going?'

'Three leaders, including you. Ben, of course. Tom too, if he's back. Tom's very keen on caving, and gets the kids interested. Good for them, you see. So many come from unhappy homes. With his dad working abroad a lot of the time he's on his own except for his grandparents, so it's good for Tom too.'

He stopped for a moment to take a puff of breath, and then set off again, his short legs striding swiftly through the heather. Lauren marvelled that with his weight he could keep up such a cracking pace.

She thought about Tom without saying anything. She had Dad, but Tom must get lonely sometimes. He had the grandparents, though.

She hung back a little and Richard looked back. Kindness and understanding shone from his eyes. All at once she felt like telling him everything. She bit her lip, undecided.

'Sometimes it helps to talk if you have a problem,' he said, his voice gentle, as she caught up with him again.

She knew it did, and she had tried both with Vicki and Ben.

Suddenly Richard let out a shout that set the hillside ringing. 'Lunch in ten minutes over the other side of the hill. Start as soon as you get there.'

Everyone's pace quickened. You would think that they'd had no sustenance for days, Lauren thought, as she watched them disappear into the distance.

Richard's eyes crinkled at her as he smiled. 'I'd like to help if you'll let me.'

Lauren stared at him, seeing a small, round, elderly man in blue shorts and white shirt, who looked odd and funny with his rucksack bumping high on his back. Yet there was dignity about him, too, that commanded the respect of everyone who knew him. She felt enveloped in his understanding, yet he could have no idea of what was troubling her.

He removed his rucksack and undid it. 'Hungry?' He took out his packet of sandwiches and a can of Coke. 'It's early, but who cares?' He threw himself down on the ground and sat with his short legs stuck out in front of him. He began to undo the packet as if food was the only thing he cared about.

Lauren sat down too, and got out her ration of food. As she ate she began to talk, and before she realised it she had poured out everything. There was something about the stout figure at her side that made the telling easy.

Richard wasn't smiling now. He wasn't even eating. He sat with his half-eaten sandwich poised in the air.

'So,' he said. 'Decision time. You're regretting not agreeing to meet the boy. Is that it?'

Lauren shot him an agonised look. 'Yes . . . no. I don't know.' She dug the toe of one trainer into a patch of loose soil, and made a little hole. She watched the earth slide back in as she removed her foot. 'You see, I don't want Dad to be hurt by this.' It was like talking to herself . . . saying out loud that Mum had hurt her. Nothing should be kept hidden . . . why had Mum done this to her?'

'And you think your meeting this boy would hurt your dad?'

Lauren's eyes were large in her pale face. She didn't answer for a moment. 'You don't hurt people if you can help it,' she said at last, slowly.

Richard smiled. 'Sometimes it's hard to know when you are hurting people. No one knows exactly how someone else feels. We can only do what we feel to be right.'

'I can see that.' Lauren looked away from him to the bracken on the brow of the hill. It had felt right to apologize to Grace, and to Ben too. She had felt better immediately because of it. Tom had felt it right to go to York for his grandparents' Golden Wedding celebrations.

Turning to Richard again, she saw that his eyes were warm with sympathy. 'Tom didn't want to hurt his grandparents,' she said. 'That's why he left. Dad took him to the station at Harrogate. He was late back.'

'He's a kind chap, your dad. Like Tom himself.'

'Tom was kind to me on that first hike,' Lauren said, smiling as she remembered Tom's pretence about the reservoir not being on the map. Just testing, he'd said. He'd asked her about Dad, too, and been particularly interested in what she said. Testing?

She opened her eyes wide as a shattering thought shot into her mind. 'You said Tom's dad works abroad. Had he always . . . since Tom was a baby, I mean? Did Tom live abroad too?'

'You'll have to ask him that yourself, love. I only know that his base is at his grandparents' home in York. I expect you know that he's at college in Newcastle in term time, and helps out with our church group when he's there. But I don't know any more than that.'

She stared at him in silence, and the hillside seemed to ring with such important information she could hardly breathe. She didn't have to discover any more. She knew.

She knew, too, with a little tingling sensation, why Tom had failed to return to the group at Alderdale. It was because of her reaction to the request in the solicitor's letter. Why hadn't she thought of something so obvious before? Stephen Thomas Harmer, she thought. Tom.

'His surname,' she whispered. 'I never asked you . . .'

'Harmer. Tom Harmer.'

She leapt up. 'I must get back, at once, I need to telephone. Do you know Tom's grandparents' telephone number?'

Richard got to his feet, surprisingly agile for his bulk. 'Harmer's the name, W. J. Harmer of Stone Street, York. It's in the book.'

She rammed her uneaten sandwiches into her rucksack, and took a deep, determined breath. 'I'm going back on my own.'

'But why, love?'

'I'm going to make sure Tom comes caving with us tomorrow. I'll be all right. See you later. And . . . thanks!'

Richard looked perplexed but he made no effort to stop her, and she was grateful. The last she saw of him was when he reached the skyline and disappeared over the top to join the rest of the group. She hoped he managed to eat the rest of his lunch before they all moved on.

Only one thought filled her mind now as she raced along the shore of the lake. 'Oh, please let Tom be there at his grandparents' house . . . please, *please* let him be there!'

The last person she wanted to see was Joanna with her arms full of tarpaulin coming down the track towards her.

'What are you doing here?' Joanna demanded. 'What's wrong? An accident . . . ?'

'No, no!' Lauren gasped out. 'Nothing like that.'

Joanna deposited her bulky cargo on the path at her feet. 'D'you want your dad? He's up in the office.' She looked slightly flushed, and her eyes were bright. Her broad shoulders pulled the sleeves of her yellow T-shirt up to the top of her arms, and there was a distinct line where suntan ended and white skin began.

Lauren stood poised, ready to leap past her. 'I want to use the phone, quickly.'

Joanna raised her bushy eyebrows.

'Please!' Lauren cried desperately. 'It's important, and I've got to be on my own to do it.'

'I *see*.'

She didn't, but she thought she did. Lauren threw her an agitated look, frantic to get rid of her. 'I can't stop.'

'All right, all right, sorry I spoke.' Joanna bent to heave up the tarpaulin again, but then thought better of it. 'Tell you what, Lauren. I'll act as decoy if you like and get your dad out of the office for you. That'll give you time.'

Lauren took a quick breath, and looked at her suspiciously.

Joanna's brown eyes lit up as she smiled. 'Go and tell him I need him down by the boats.'

Lauren hesitated. This was the first time Joanna had

offered to do something for her.

Joanna shrugged. 'Oh well, if you don't want to . . .' This time she hoisted the tarpaulin up on one hip. 'Quarrel with Richard, did you? I must say, you girls! But if you don't want my help . . .'

'I do,' Lauren cried, surprising herself. 'Thanks, Joanna.'

It could make no difference really. Dad was his own person. He'd make up his own mind about Joanna one way or the other. No one else would influence him. He wasn't like that. She had to trust him.

He looked none too pleased when she delivered the message. 'Joanna wants to see me down at the lake? Are you sure, lass? She was here a minute ago.'

Lauren nodded. 'Quite sure, Dad. Can I use the phone?' She couldn't quite hide her pleasure at his frown of annoyance as he got up from his desk and went out and shut the door.

Quickly she found the telephone directory. Harmer was a common name and she had to go through the list twice before she found the number she wanted.

As she dialled the number her hand shook. The ringing tone seemed to go on for ever. Then a voice spoke.

She hadn't expected it would be Tom. His grandfather, perhaps, or grandmother saying they'd give a message, but not Tom himself.

For a moment she didn't know what to say, and then it came rushing out. 'This is Lauren Wainwright. Please can you come back? They need you here. We're going caving tomorrow, and . . .' A horrible sense of panic rose in her in case he wouldn't come.

'Tomorrow?' His voice sounded firm and very near.

'Tomorrow,' she repeated faintly. 'Please come. I want you to.'

116

'All right,' he said. 'See you tomorrow.'

And that was all. Lauren crept down the steps, feeling deflated. Dad down in the boatyard unnecessarily, Joanna doing her a favour, Richard on the hike with the group on his own . . . and all because she had to phone Tom to tell him . . . what? Nothing, really. She hadn't said *why* she wanted him to come back. Not the real heart-stopping reason . . .

She jumped as she almost bumped into Vicki.

'For goodness sake, Lauren, you look like death! What are *you* doing back so soon? Come and sit down if you don't feel well. I'll make you a coffee.

It was a relief to let Vicki take over, and the coffee was welcome. What would Vicki say if she knew what she had just done? But she wouldn't tell her. She had to see this thing through on her own.

It was the longest day Lauren had ever spent. She wandered up to the cottage and then down again in time to join in lunch, which was eaten on the balcony with Dad, Grace and Vicki. Then after the washing up was done, and the tables laid for the evening meal, she went down to the lake to see if there was something she could do to help Ben now that the sailing group he was with today was back on shore.

He stood in the middle of the group of four in the boatyard, waving one hand as he explained something to them. His denim shorts were frayed at the knees, and there was a muddy patch down the side of his leg.

Ben saw her as the members of the group dispersed to see to the boats they had been using. He smiled slightly, and then frowned. He handed her a shackle. 'Look after that for a minute, and don't drop it. Some-one's got one missing on the boom end. It's a wonder the sail didn't come down on them.'

As she took the small metal item Lauren marvelled that such a small thing should be so important. Small things were important in her life, too. Tiny things that made big ones happen . . . like going with Richard today and, without his having said much at all, her realising something that was vital to her.

'Tom'll be back tomorrow,' she said.

Ben shot her a penetrating look and then started wiping the inside of the boat with a muddy sponge. He squeezed the water out onto the grass and then threw the sponge down. 'That'll please you,' he said, bending over the boat and lifting out the rudder.

It didn't sound as if the news pleased him though. He kept his back turned towards her all the time he was seeing to the boat. She couldn't see the expression on his face but from the line of his shoulders she could see that he would have liked to say more about it if he had dared. For a brief moment she was tempted to tell him. But there was nothing to tell . . . yet.

Ben placed the rudder next to the tiller on the grass. Overhead the stays rattled rhythmically against the masts.

'You said about caving tomorrow,' she said at last.

He straightened. 'Why not?'

So he wasn't going to say any more . . . about what she needed to take, where exactly they were going, or anything? He wasn't going to help her at all.

'See you, then,' she said, turning away.

It was Joanna who told her something of what it was really like underground. 'No one can explain exactly . . . you have to find out how it feels for yourself,' she said as they helped clear away the evening meal. 'It's wonderful, Lauren, out of this world. It changes you, somehow.'

'But suppose I don't know what to do?'

Joanna laughed. 'Ben'll explain to all of you before you go down.' She picked up a pile of plates and looked at Lauren thoughtfully. 'You'll get soaking wet, and it's always cold deep down. Take a change of clothes with you. Ben'll sort out the helmets and things. You say Tom's coming back?'

Lauren nodded and looked away, not wanting to see the inquisitive expression she knew was in Joanna's eyes. She had enough to cope with without that.

'You're not apprehensive, are you?' Joanna threw over her shoulder as she carried the plates to the hatch. Back again, she rattled the clean knives and forks together before putting them on one side.

'I'm all right,' Lauren said.

Later Richard had a word with her as they went down to the tents together to start the evening activities. 'It's good news about Tom returning,' he said, smiling at her. He didn't look hot now, and the green shirt he had on flapped across his chest. He seemed to have forgotten the way she had flown off so suddenly when she was supposed to be on the hike with him and the group.

'Tom's coming caving tomorrow,' she said.

His eyes twinkled. 'You're not still worried about going underground?'

She shook her head. She wasn't, now. Going down into the black depths of the earth held no terrors at all for her. What was frightening was the thought of meeting Tom again now that she knew who he really was.

~13~

Ben glanced at his watch for the third time. Lauren, looking his way, saw how pale he looked and wondered if he would cancel the caving trip today. Even she was beginning to think Tom wouldn't get here in time.

She sat quite still in the back of the van. Around her was noise and excited chatter from the eight others who were in the caving group, but she had no feelings at all . . . just a numb ache.

Then a cheer went up. The solitary figure coming down the track from the road didn't look like Tom, but she knew it was. He seemed taller, and the woolly hat he wore today was blue. His fair hair was completely hidden.

Willing hands helped haul first his rucksack and then himself into the back of the van. As Ben started up the engine and moved off, everybody was clamouring to know where Tom had been.

Before the van swung round the bend in the track Lauren caught a quick glimpse out of the back window of Dad waving them off, with Grace close at his side.

She pressed herself back into a corner, glad that there was no necessity to say anything to Tom. What could she say, anyway, in the midst of all this crush?

The rough, jolting journey seemed endless, but at last Ben pulled up in a lay-by off a narrow lane. They all scrambled out.

Lauren hadn't known quite what to expect, but certainly not the small, rocky hole at the base of a limestone outcrop, at the bottom of the sloping field over the other side of the wall.

'Have we got to go in there?' she gasped, as Ben started to unload the helmets from the van and hand them out.

Tom was already over the wall. As she followed the others Lauren held back a little. Ben, his own helmet slung over one arm, joined her and together they went down across the squelchy grass. He looked straight ahead, not speaking.

'Get your helmets on and the lights checked,' he told them all when they got there. 'You know the drill. Single file, each keeping a close watch on those in front and behind you. Understood?'

'Understood!' they all shouted.

'I'll put Tom in front until we get to the rope bridge,' Ben said quietly to Lauren. 'He'll explain what to do as you go along. Then you next, and I'll come at the end. All right?'

In the cold darkness Lauren clambered over boulders until they petered out and the ground was smooth rock. Every now and again her helmet crashed against the rock above, echoing inside her head. She thought she heard rushing water.

Immediately ahead of her Tom's reassuring voice encouraged her on, and she felt water beneath her feet.

'The river,' Tom said. 'Stand still and wait for the others to catch up.'

Lauren moved her head so that the light shone downwards. 'I'm glad you came back,' she said with a rush, glad that she couldn't see him. 'When I found out who you were . . .'

Tom's voice was warm. 'How did you know it was me?'

She shrugged, and then realised he couldn't see in the darkness. 'From what Richard said . . . I guessed.'

'I thought your dad did too, that night he gave me a lift to the station, but I wasn't sure. I wondered what he would do.'

Lauren thought about it, remembering how late back Dad had been because he'd sat in the car at the top of the track, thinking. But he'd never said, not once. Had he guessed, and kept quiet?

She couldn't say any more now because the rest of them were catching up, with a scraping of boots as they moved along the black tunnel. She was glad, though, that she had said something to Tom at last. Down here in this dark world it seemed right and natural to talk to him about it.

Ben's voice rang out, explaining that they'd soon reach the pool but telling them first to shine their helmet lights round the cave they were in. A gasp of wonder escaped from everyone as they did as he said and their helmet lights made patterns on the rocky roof. Then Tom, ahead of her, splashed into the pool.

To her surprise Lauren felt no sense of apprehension as she followed him, and no sense of the coldness of the water, either. As she clambered out at the other side she felt a glow of happiness.

She smiled at Tom and saw his eyes shine back at her

in the light from her helmet. 'Like it?' he asked.

'Yes, oh yes.'

'I wasn't going to come to Alderdale this year because of the Golden Wedding,' he said. 'Until I discovered the name of the new warden, and that his daughter'd be here too. You.'

'The name . . . how did you know?'

'Your uncle wrote, you see, and told me your name. It's not very common . . . so I took a chance. Just testing.'

'Uncle Dave's your uncle too.' She couldn't see him smile as he turned his head away, but she felt that he did. 'But . . . you didn't come back?'

'It wasn't fair, was it? Not unless you wanted it too, and I knew you didn't.'

'The solicitor's letter?'

'That's it.'

They moved on again, this time towards the mud slide that Tom explained took them further down into the earth. He sat down, letting himself go into blackness. The smell from the muddy slime bit at Lauren's nostrils as she followed and then stood waiting for the rest of them.

She thought about what Tom had said. Having him as her half-brother was all right. But that wasn't the problem. It was Mum. Her mother hadn't wanted them to meet, so how could it be right for them to get together now?

'What was your life like?' she asked.

She heard him slide one boot across the wet rock. 'Dad knew he could never have another child of his own. He told me that. I was the only one. When Mum and Dad split up, you see, he was desperate to take me with him, and they thought it was best for *me*, both of them. The family firm, carrying on the name . . . and *he* could give me a good home. And it worked out. We went to Belgium for a time, and he still goes there. He married Mum . . . my new Mum . . . she died last year . . . and Gran and Gramp are lovely people.'

'Get a move on in the front there!' someone called, and they were off again.

The light from Lauren's head searched out all the secret indents in the rock as they continued on down the narrowing passage, with the roar of the river sounding above their heads now. When at last they came to the rope bridge Ben halted them all to count the helmet lights, to make sure no one had got lost along the way.

'The bridge is a metre long, and made of rope,' he was saying, but Lauren could hardly take it in for the emotions swirling in her head. She tried hard to concentrate. 'No need to panic, anyone. It's quite safe if you do as you're told. I'll take Lauren over first and down the rift, and then come back for the rest of you one at a time. Tom, stay till last.'

He stepped onto the rope, and she heard his voice ahead of her. 'One step on it, slide your feet along, then leave go of the rock and take my hand.'

She took a deep breath, and did as he said. Carefully she slid her feet along until she felt solid rock.

'Sit at my side,' came his reassuring voice in the darkness. 'Wriggle yourself along with your feet on the rock and your knees supporting you.'

It sounded horrific, but there was no escape. She just had to do it.

'All right, Lauren?' His voice sounded remote, and then she realised he had dropped himself down a narrow black fissure at her feet. 'Come on. I'll catch you.'

Her mouth dry, she slithered down through the crack

with her helmet clashing on the sides, to solid ground. She let out a gasp of relief.

'Wait round the corner,' Ben said as he prepared to climb up again. 'It'll take some time to get the rest through.' His voice sounded cold.

For a moment she stood still, her heart thudding. It seemed just like the narrow gate she had read about in Matthew's gospel. She thought about the words she had read: 'The gate to life is narrow and the way that leads to it is hard, and there are few people who find it.' Now that she was physically through the narrow rift she felt a glow of freedom that made her smile in relief.

She found a rock for a seat, and sat with her back pressed hard against the rocky wall to wait. And now she had time to think and space, plenty of black space.

She had never been completely alone before. Not like this. She might have been the only one down here in this subterranean world. Suppose she was? Suppose the rest decided to go back the other way without her? But Tom had remembered her . . . had wanted to meet her and make himself known. He wouldn't forget her now . . . or she him.

Mum had wanted to do the best for Tom. And wasn't it true?

The rock at her back cut into her flesh and she moved a little to ease it. Mum had wanted to do her best for herself too. If was the way she thought best . . . to keep the past to herself and not tell her. It was for her sake, and not her own. Mum was that sort of person. A sob broke in Lauren's throat. Mum didn't know she would die . . . that the accident on the motorway was going to happen. Things were different now, because Mum had died.

Tears welled up in Lauren's eyes and she let them fall.

They seemed to ease something deep down that she had tried so hard to bury and forget. But not any more. Now she had no need to, and somehow Richard's words at the service by the lakeside had a lot to do with it. She remembered, too, her desperate prayer that her brother wouldn't come searching for her when she wanted to be left in peace. But she *had* wanted it, in the end, and now that it had happened she had peace. Her prayers were answered.

'In Jesus is life, now and for ever,' Richard had said at the lakeside service. It was true. She knew now for certain that this was true for herself, and always would be. Sudden glorious warmth flooded through her. She had felt a sudden glow of freedom as she came physically through the narrow rift just now. But this was even better! Loving Jesus brought freedom . . . true freedom.

She heard a voice . . . Ben's. They'd be here soon, Ben and the next to come down the rift with him.

You didn't know how other people felt . . . how could you know unless they told you? With a sudden blinding realisation she understood what was wrong with Ben. Not anger at her disagreement with Grace, not that at all, but unhappiness because she, Lauren, seemed to prefer Tom to himself. There was a lot she hadn't understood, but now she saw it clearly.

She stood up at the sound of something landing heavily, the scrape of boots on rock and the relieved babble of someone else safely through. They seemed to come quickly after that, and it was time to move off again with Tom in the lead.

The roar of water was loud now.

'The underground waterfall!' Tom shouted.

It was like climbing a waterlogged staircase, and Lauren splashed water onto her face and then gasped with the freshness of it.

'Daylight ahead,' Tom called out, his voice cheerful.

The message was passed back, and she felt the exuberant relief of all of them. It felt good emerging into bright, startling daylight again. She blinked, smiling at the excited antics of the group members rolling about on the grass. Only she and Ben and Tom stood a little to one side, watching them.

Tom wrenched off his helmet, threw it in the air and caught it. His hair was fairer than hers but grew in the same way off the peak. Why hadn't she noticed it before?

She turned to Ben and saw that he was watching them, a slight frown creasing his forehead. He undid the strap on his own helmet, removed it and ran his hand through his flattened hair so that it stood up in dark peaks. His eyes looked very bright.

She moved to stand beside him. 'Ben,' she said, her voice vibrant. 'It was great. I wouldn't have missed it for anything. I can't wait to come with you again!'

There was a moment's silence as her voice seemed to hang in the air. Then such an expression of sweetness illuminated Ben's face that she felt tears spring to her eyes once more.

There were just the two of them standing among the rocks now. The others had moved off, and Tom with them. There was explaining to do, lots of it, but that would come later. What was important was this feeling of lightness, this removing of the burden of having to forgive Mum . . . but she hadn't any more, had she? There wasn't anything to forgive . . .

'So you're really glad you came?' Ben asked.

Lauren took a deep breath and let it out slowly. Joanna had said caving was great, and it was. She had the clearest picture of the van setting out with herself squashed into a corner of it, and Dad standing with Grace to see them off . . . Dad and Grace? She'd think about that later.

She nodded, her eyes shining.

Ben caught hold of her hand. 'C'mon. We'd better catch up. The others'll be changed by now and ready for off.'

She'd forgotten how muddy and wet she was. She laughed and he did too as they ran, stumbling, up the rutted field.